CUT FROM THE SAME CLOTH

Other Books by Author

Life Under Construction:

The Davenport's Story

CUT FROM THE SAME CLOTH

TJ ROBINSON

Copyright © 2018 by TJ Robinson

All rights reserved. No part of this book may be reproduced or transmitted in any form or by any means without written permission of the author.

First Printing, 2018

This is a work of fiction. Names, characters, businesses, organizations, places, events, and incidents are the product of the author's imagination or are used fictionally. Any resemblance to actual persons, living or dead, is entirely coincidental.

Cover design by: TJ Robinson

Editing: ddianeott.com

Cover Images: pngtree.com

Dedication

This book is dedicated to my sister Pamela F. Johnson. Although she did not have breast cancer, she lost her battle to pancreatic cancer.

You are truly missed. May you continue to rest in peace, PJ.

I would also like to dedicate this book to my sister friends who are breast cancer survivors. May God continue to bless you! You know who you are...

ACKNOWLEDGEMENT

I would like to acknowledge my husband, Michael Robinson for being a wonderful and understanding husband during this process.

Table of Contents

- CHAPTER ONE 1
- CHAPTER TWO 11
- CHAPTER THREE 24
- CHAPTER FOUR 33
- CHAPTER FIVE 43
- CHAPTER SIX 53
- CHAPTER SEVEN 66
- CHAPTER EIGHT 81
- CHAPTER NINE 89
- CHAPTER TEN 102
- CHAPTER ELEVEN 113
- CHAPTER TWELVE 123
- CHAPTER THIRTEEN 133
- CHAPTER FOURTEEN 145
- CHAPTER FIFTEEN 154
- CHAPTER SIXTEEN 166
- CHAPTER SEVENTEEN 176
- CHAPTER EIGHTEEN 188
- CHAPTER NINETEEN 196
- CHAPTER TWENTY 208
- CHAPTER TWENTY-ONE 221
- CHAPTER TWENTY-TWO 227
- CHAPTER TWENTY-THREE 234
- CHAPTER TWENTY – FOUR 243

CHAPTER TWENTY-FIVE 253

CHAPTER TWENTY-SIX 260

CHAPTER TWENTY-SEVEN 267

CHAPTER TWENTY-EIGHT 275

CHAPTER TWENTY-NINE 283

CHAPTER THIRTY 291

CHAPTER THIRTY-ONE 299

CHAPTER THIRTY-TWO 307

CHAPTER THIRTY-THREE 316

CHAPTER THIRTY-FOUR 326

CHAPTER THIRTY- FIVE 337

CHAPTER THIRTY-SIX 350

CHAPTER THIRTY-SEVEN 361

CHAPTER THIRTY-EIGHT 368

CHAPTER THIRTY-NINE 377

Chapter One

This was the beginning of the end. The day Piper Jackson-Evans would tell her husband that life for them would never be the same. That they were in for the fight of their lives.

Reminiscing about her wedding day, she recalled how handsome Scott had looked in his charcoal-black tuxedo, fresh haircut and smooth shave. How he had shed tears upon her entrance into the vast church. How he had shined bright in the shadows of the stained-glass windows. He was happy the day had finally come when she would become his wife. She remembered the words they shared: *Till death do us part.*

She thought her conversation with Scott would be like her wedding day. They would hold each other in a tight embrace and cry together. She thought they would make a plan so that she would get the best of care. She thought Scott would say, "I'll be with you, PJ. We will get through this together."

Piper had it — she had cancer. The lump in her breast was malignant. The doctor was hopeful, but Piper was skeptical. "Early detection and an aggressive treatment plan, is the key to your progress, as long as you don't capitulate," Dr. Cheung had told her.

Piper was a nurse. She administered medication daily, but she was not good at taking it. *How will I be able to deal with being a patient?* she thought.

The conversation with Scott did not go as planned. Instead, she felt as if she had received another diagnosis: that she had two forms of cancer and that one was Scott. He was outraged.

He told her that he didn't want the responsibility of taking care of her while she was sick. "I don't want the burden of seeing you lie in bed helpless and carrying on like you can't do anything for yourself. Cleaning you when you are dirty. Having to take off from work so that you can go to your appointments. I'm not doing it. I guess now we know whose fault it was that you never conceived. Your cancer cells are probably the reason why we never had children," he had griped. "You have enough family to take care of you, anyway. Your mom and sisters can do it. I'm not going to, PJ. We're done."

Piper was stunned, she felt embarrassed and confused. She realized at that moment that she had wasted five years of marriage to a selfish, hateful man. His reaction came out of nowhere. She thought her husband loved her. She knew things were a little strained between them, but she didn't think it was all that bad. After his rant, Piper said in a very monotone voice, "I've never needed you. I didn't when we got married, and I definitely don't now. You're right, I do have my family."

"Yeah, I know. That's mainly my problem," Scott said as he left the house.

Piper went to see her best friend, her sister Harmony, to give her the news. They had suspected it when she first found the lump, but PJ wanted to receive the news from the doctor alone. She would not allow Harmony to go with her. The two were the closest in age out of her four siblings. Her older siblings would refer to them as "menopausal babies." Now that she was twenty-five, and Harmony was twenty-four, she thought that they would give up on referring to them as the latecomers. But her brothers still considered them "late" babies.

"I got the 'C,' Harm," she said as she opened the heavy door to Harmony's condominium. "This is it. I'm going to die. Thank God I went to church. Well, sometimes, anyways, and paid my tithes. Sometimes," PJ rambled.

"Are you giving up just like that?" Harmony asked. "You're a fighter. You have the faith of Abraham. You can beat this, PJ. This is what you know. You're a nurse, and you've seen the good and bad. You've talked to survivors.

We will get through this, PJ. Together." Harmony wrapped her arms around her sister's neck, and hugged her as they sat in the entryway of the condominium, on the cold hardwood floor.

Piper hugged her younger sister tightly and said, "You have always been there for me, Harm. Thank you. You're right. I have my family. I don't need Scott. I will fight, and I will win."

"What do you mean, you don't need Scott? You told him, right?" Harmony asked.

"Yeah, I did. I don't want to go into details right now, but we're done. It's over. He bailed on me, Harm."

"Oh, PJ. I am so sorry. You have us, your family, and no matter what you go through, we will be there for you. All of us: Daphne, Brock, Davon, Mom and Dad."

"Thanks, Harm," PJ said solemnly. "Will you stand with me when I tell Mom and Dad?"

"Of course. But you know we do things together. You need to gather the clan and we'll all tell them together."

"All right. I'll call everyone tonight and we can meet at my place tomorrow after everyone's off from work."

"Daphne included?" Harmony asked, worried.

Daphne was the eldest of them all. She was exactly like their mother: emotional, but all business and pompous. She had battled breast cancer years earlier and was now in remission.

"Yeah, I'll call her first. Listen to her lecture and make sure she knows I have burial insurance and my final wishes are in order. Brock and Davon will be easy to talk to, but I'm not sure if I want to involve their wives. Not yet, at least. You know Renée. She thinks everything is hereditary. She may want Rena to get a mammogram."

"Rena's ten!"

"Exactly."

Later that evening, Piper returned to a house that sounded hollow upon the closing of the wood door. She entered the spacious family room. The fifty-five–inch television that had been mounted on the wall, gone. The entertainment center, missing. From the family room, she could see the side-by-side stainless steel refrigerator, with a note affixed to it with a magnet. It was from Scott:

PJ,

I am truly sorry that our life together did not go as planned. I just could not do it anymore PJ. We got married far too soon. I wish you the best.

Scott

"A freakin' note on the fridge is all I get? 'I wish you the BEST'?" Piper yelled. She grabbed her cell phone from her purse and called Harmony.

"Harm?" she said. "He's gone."

"Who's gone?" Harmony asked.

"Scott. He took the entertainment system, and all of his clothes are gone."

"What? PJ, what is going on?"

"He left me, Harm," Piper cried.

"I'm on my way." Harmony hung up the phone.

It took Harmony fifteen minutes to drive to Piper's house. The Jacksons all kept keys to each other's homes for emergencies. She opened the front door with her key and entered. She found Piper sitting in front of the fireplace in the family room, on a black rug made of faux fur, sipping a glass of wine.

"PJ," she said softly. "Are you all right?"

"Well, let's replay my day. I found out I have cancer, my husband left me and blamed me for us not having children. No, Harmony, I am not all right. I feel as if I am going to lose my mind. I thought I was strong. I thought I could handle this. But I can't. I have a big empty house with nothing in it but me."

"I'm here, too, PJ. I will always be here for you." She sat next to Piper, took the glass from her hand, and put Piper's head on her lap. "I don't think this can wait until tomorrow," Harmony said. "We're calling everyone over tonight."

"It's too late. They have their family and their jobs. No need to do this tonight," Piper said.

"What is it that Daddy always say? 'We are family. We are cut from the same cloth. Nothing comes before us but God.' I'm calling now," Harmony said.

First, she phoned Daphne, who was thirty minutes away. She knew it would take her all night to get dressed. "Gym suits are for the gym, and jeans are too casual and I don't own a pair," so Daphne had said many times. Harmony informed her that PJ was having a crisis and Daphne assured her that she would be there directly. Brock Jr., the eldest brother, lived nearby and said he was enroute. Davon, on the other hand, was standing outside the door. Daphne had called him after she hung up with Harmony.

He knocked on the door while entering with his key. "Hello, it's me, Davon." He noticed his sisters in a huddle with Piper's head on Harmony's lap. "That bad?" he said. "Well, get it together. Daphne said she was calling Mom and Dad after she phoned me."

"Get up, PJ. Let's go to the bathroom and get your face together." Harmony grabbed Piper by her elbow and rushed up the stairs.

As Davon looked around the room, he noticed the missing entertainment system and television. "Hey, PJ, were you robbed?"

Chapter Two

Within an hour, the Jackson family had assembled in Piper's family room. She was not prepared to tell her parents, but thanks to Daphne, she had no other choice. As usual, their father, Brock Sr., was at the head of the seating arrangements. He sat in the large, black leather recliner, and her mother, Madeline, sat on the black leather sofa. Piper sat between her brothers, Brock Jr. and Davon, on the larger sofa so that they could comfort her. Daphne sat next to her mother, and Harmony sat on the beige chaise lounge that rested on the faux fur rug in front of the fireplace.

Mr. Jackson noticed the obvious — that things were missing from the living space — and could only shake his head. He spoke first, in his baritone voice. "So, were you robbed?" he asked.

Before Piper could answer, her mother said, "Have you call the police?"

"She wasn't robbed..." Harmony tried to say. Before she could finish her sentence, her dad gave her the "I was talking to PJ" look.

Everyone recognized Mr. Jackson as the head of this family. He raised them all to be respectful to their elders and to love one another. Harmony retreated.

"Dad, Mom, I have so much to tell you," Piper said.

"Well, let's get started," Mr. Jackson said.

"I found out today that I have breast cancer."

Mrs. Jackson looked away. She could not bear the thought of another daughter going through what Daphne went through to get rid of that terrible disease. But she knew if there was a chance for her survival, Piper would have to do just that.

"Come here, Piper," her father said. He sat her on his lap and held her tight.

Her mother went to her and said, "We can beat this, Piper. We did it once and we will do it again." Everyone gathered around her and gave her hugs, one at a time, to comfort her.

"Piper?" Daphne said. "Now, I've been there. I'm living proof you can and will survive. Now, tomorrow we'll go over all your personal ..."

Harmony stopped Daphne mid-sentence and said, "I got it, Daph. I have all her information. No need to discuss that right now, okay?"

Looking defeated, Daphne said, "I see."

Mr. Jackson cleared his throat. The family did not know if he was trying to get their attention, or if he was clearing it from the tears he had shed for his daughter. Either way, he had their full attention. "Piper, I am sorry you have to fight this battle. But you are not alone. We are a family that believe in miracles. We believe God can get us through all trials and tribulations. You stay strong in your belief, and hold on to the love you have in this room, and that will get us through this." Without missing a beat, he suddenly said, "Where's Scott?"

"Well, that's another issue," Piper said.

"Did he remove the belongings from the house?" her father asked.

"Yes," she responded.

"Did they belong to him?" he questioned.

"He pays the credit card bill, so I guess, yes, it was his," she said.

"It was community property," her mother said angrily.

"It was material and can be replaced," Mr. Jackson stated.

"Where is he?" Brock Jr. added.

"I don't know. He left and isn't coming back," Piper said.

Daphne put her hands to her throat as if she had just realized her diamond necklace was missing. "Oh, no, Piper. What are you going to do without your husband? If Sherwin had not been there for me, I don't know what I would have done. You need to make amends. He will be so helpful to you during this process and you need that support."

Mrs. Jackson nodded her head in agreement as Daphne spoke.

"She has her family," Mr. Jackson sternly stated. "What happened between Piper and Scott is between Piper and Scott." He looked at Daphne, then his wife, and said, "I want it to stay between Piper and Scott. Am I understood?"

"Yes, Daddy," Daphne responded.

Mrs. Jackson said, "Brock, you know my only concern is for Piper and her well-being."

"I can manage, Mom. I will downsize if need be. I don't think I can stay in this big house alone, anyway," Piper said.

"When does the treatment begin?" Mrs. Jackson asked.

"I have blood work tomorrow and am scheduled to take a tour of the facility. I'll see Dr. Cheung then," Piper said.

"Will they insert a port or will it be done through an I.V.?" Daphne asked.

"I won't know until my visit. Dr. Cheung is the head Oncologist at Lincoln Memorial Oncology Center, in the Valley. They are first in the country in cancer research. He's very optimistic that I'll recover. Some people say the treatment center is nice and relaxing. A resort-like atmosphere, to make you feel comfortable."

Brock Jr. noticed the inadvertent tremble in Piper's voice, and held her hand as she spoke. He whispered in her ear and asked if they could speak after the family meeting. Piper agreed. Piper and Harmony often looked to their older siblings as parental figures. She knew Brock Jr. had a lot on his plate and that the amount of help he could offer might be limited.

When the family meeting concluded, everyone walked outside to bid their farewells to one another. Brock Jr. returned to the house and sat with Piper on the sofa. He put his arm around her and said, "Do you need me to speak with Scott?"

"No, Brock. I'm fine with his decision to leave," she replied.

"You know I'm here for you, when you need me. Any time, day or night."

"Thank you, big brother."

Brock held her and kissed her on her forehead. He asked, "Will you be okay in the house, alone, tonight?"

Piper chuckled and replied, "Yes, I'll be fine. Go home to Ashlyn."

She walked him to the door and before he reached his car, he pivoted and looked at his sister. "There's something not quite right about Scott's leaving this way."

Piper looked at him and asked, "What do you mean?"

"Not now. I don't like accusations, so until I know for sure, I'll keep my thoughts to myself. Goodnight, PJ, and try and get some rest. Today has been a trying day."

Piper returned to the hollow home. She sat at the breakfast nook and finished a half bottle of wine and tried to recall how her family had responded to her news.

Exhausted, she started up the steps. She stopped when she heard a key turn in the lock on the front door. Though her siblings all had keys to each other's homes, they respected the spouses and would knock before entering. She thought, for a second, that maybe Scott was returning. But why would he come back? He had obviously brought the largest U-Haul truck he could find to the front door and got all of his belongings the first time around. She quickly trotted up the steps to prevent him from seeing her, but stopped when she heard someone say, "Where you going, Auntie PJ?"

She turned and saw Rena, her ten-year-old niece, with her brother Davon and his wife Renée, hauling sleeping bags and suitcases as if they were on their way to a camping trip.

"Hey Niecey!" Piper descended the staircase and Rena ran and gave her the biggest hug and kiss. "Hey

Renée!" she said to her sister-in-law. They hugged and kissed each other on the cheek. As she released Renée, she noticed a tear floating down Renée's left eye and whispered, "I'm okay. Really, I am." Piper looked over to Davon quizzically.

"I hope it's okay if we camp out in your family room," Davon said.

"And why do you need to camp out in my family room?" Piper asked.

Davon approached her and said, "On my way home, I phoned Renée, gave her the news, and she told Rena that you were a little sick and Rena suggested we come by. And I said, 'Well, let's stay the night.' I told her that her Uncle Scott had to leave town and that you would be alone tonight. Rena thought it was a great idea. She said you always play nurse to others. Now we can nurse to you back to good health."

"Oh, Rena, come here, baby. Auntie's fine. Thank you, sweetie. I love you," she said and hugged her tightly.

"I love you, too, Auntie PJ."

"You guys are welcome to stay the night, but I'm going upstairs to let Calgon take me away."

"You need anything?" Renée asked.

"No, Renée, but I do appreciate the gesture. Thank you," Piper said.

Davon and Rena moved the furniture to make room for their sleeping bags. Piper shook her head. "You know I have two guest bedrooms? You are more than welcome to sleep in either one."

"Good," Renée said. "I haven't slept on a floor in years."

"Hey Rena, let's sleep in the bedrooms. We can still put the sleeping bags on top of the beds so it will still feel like a sleepover," Davon said.

"Naw, I rather sleep down here and watch — Hey Auntie, where's the big TV?"

Piper couldn't take it anymore. She continued upstairs to her bedroom. She went into her ensuite and shut the door without looking back. She turned on the bathwater, dropped in a few teaspoons of Calgon. She enjoyed the steam on her face. The water soothed her feet as she stepped into the Jacuzzi tub. She soaked for several minutes, and then turned on the jets, only to have the suds of her Calgon rise to the edge of the tub. With the sounds of R&B playing from her Bluetooth speaker, she closed her eyes. She drifted far away to near unconsciousness.

Davon knew her bath was over when the music stopped. He was used to Piper's bathing habits, having lived with her for years. He knew his sister's sanctuary was a long — very long — bath. He gave her sometime before approaching her bedroom door. He knocked and asked, "PJ, are you dressed?"

"Yes," she replied.

Davon opened the door. The fresh scent of plumeria greeted him. Piper closed her Bible as he entered. "I see old habits are hard to break," he said, trying to break the tension.

"Ha ha. Did you need something?" Piper asked.

"I wanted to come and apologize. I should have called first. But I know you don't like being alone, and I know you wouldn't want to disappoint your favorite niece, so we just came over."

Piper chuckled and said, "I don't have favorites. I have four beautiful nieces and a handsome nephew. I love them all equally."

"I know. I just want you to know that I'm here for you, PJ. I'm sure Brock will try and talk to Scott, no matter what Daddy says."

"He offered. I told him I was okay with Scott's decision."

"Piper, I have to ask. What made him leave? Does he know you're sick?"

"Davon, I know you care, and love me, but I don't have the strength to deal with this right now. Can we talk about it later? I promise I will tell you all about it. I promise."

"Pinky promise?" he said as he held up his right pinky for her to grab with hers.

"You know it!" she said. "Go join your family."

"You are my family, and I think you need me a little more than they do right now," Davon told her.

Davon sat on the bed next to Piper and held her. "It's okay to cry. Here's my shoulder."

Piper looked him in his eyes and cried. "Thank you, little brother."

"Hey, I'm older than you." He held her until she fell asleep.

Chapter Three

The following morning, Piper woke to a wonderful aroma: pancakes, bacon, and eggs. Renée had decided to cook breakfast before heading off to work.

Piper had errands to run and a doctor's visit, so she more than welcomed a nice hot meal.

"Good morning, Auntie," Rena said.

"Hey sweetie. How was your sleepover?" Piper asked.

"It was okay. I wanted to watch a show on your big screen, but Daddy said it was in the shop being repaired. But the popcorn you had was really good and buttery."

"I'm glad I could offer you something," Piper replied.

Davon sat at the table eating before rushing off to work. "Hey Renée? I'll drop Rena off at school this morning and you can hang out with PJ before going into the office."

"Okay, dear. You guys have a great day and I'll see you this afternoon for lunch," Renée said.

Curious, Piper looked from Renée to Davon. She wondered what Renée could possibly say to her after Davon left. They had never been close. *I hope she doesn't want to become besties now that I'm sick,* Piper thought.

Renée saw her husband and daughter to the car and returned to the dining area, where Piper sat at the breakfast nook, having a cup of coffee.

"Would you like for me to fix you a plate?" Renée asked.

"Yes, please. Are you only working a half day today, Renée?"

"No. I'm showing two houses today and I have a three-hour break in between. Davon and I will be meeting Savannah for lunch. She and Eric are interested in buying a home and she need some information."

Knowing how involved Daphne was in her daughter Savannah's wedding to Eric McDaniel's, Piper fully expected Daphne to also take charge of the house hunting. As much as Daphne's daughters, Savannah and Sabrina, loved her, they would have preferred that their private lives go motherless.

"Ask her if she likes my house. I'm thinking about selling," Piper said.

"Are you sure? Maybe you should think about it awhile."

Renée looked at Piper with sincerity in her eyes and said, "I know that you have more sisters than you need, but I want you to know, PJ, I'm here for you if you ever need me. Davon didn't say much about Scott — just that it was over between the two of you. Are you certain you are ready to sell the house? Is your relationship that final?"

"I appreciate your concern, Renée, and thanks for the offer." Piper looked away and stared out the dining room's large bay window. Renée allowed her the solitude.

Piper had not talked about Scott much because what he said made her feel inadequate as a woman. Made her feel artificial in some way. "Renée, Scott said things to me that I cannot repeat to my family. If I share this with you, can you assure me you will not share it with Davon? I will tell him, in my time."

"Now, PJ, if it's something that I think is going to hurt you, or if someone is going to cause you harm, then I'm not sure I can keep that from your brother. I will feel obligated, as his wife, to tell him," Renée said.

"It's not that bad, Renée. I just feel so violated by him. When I told Scott that I had cancer, I felt as if I had just told a stranger. Come to think of it, a stranger may have been more sympathetic. It was like my worst enemy sticking a rusty knife in my back and twisting it with all his might. Scott and I, for the past six months, have been at odds. He wanted children, and I never conceived. He started hanging out late, not really wanting to spend quality time. Just very standoffish. I thought he was just going through a phase. His friends that are married have children and I guess he just wants them, too. Maybe I should have seen it coming, but I didn't expect the response I got when I told him I had cancer."

Piper looked at Renée. Renée's eyes were filled with tears. She was crying, balling without sound.

Renée ran to Piper and put her arms around her. "Piper, you are loved. By us, all of us. We will see you through."

"I know. My family is my backbone. But Scott was my first love. And I still love him. He blamed my cancer for us not being able to conceive a child, and that made me feel less than a woman."

"He's wrong. You are not to blame for that. It just was not meant to be. Do you think you would be able to go through what you are about to go through if you had to take care of a child? I have one and she gives me a run for my money. You are a woman, a full-fledge woman, and you are beautiful. Scott doesn't know yet what he's lost, but he will."

"Thanks, Renée, for that. I do feel better. Now I have to get ready for my day. Let me know what Savannah says and ask her not to mention it to her mom. Daphne will definitely talk her out of it."

"You're welcome, sis. Um, PJ?"

"Yeah?"

"How much about your illness do you want me to tell Rena?"

"It's up to you. You can tell her what you think she can handle. Just let her know that I don't want sympathy and to just be normal."

"She may be ten, but she's a wise ten. And she really loves you, PJ."

"I know. Davon always accuse me of playing favorites with Rena. It's not favorites. We just share a special bond."

With a broad smile, Renée replied, "If you say so."

"I have to get dress. I have an appointment in a couple of hours."

"I'll be leaving after I do the dishes," Renée said.

"And remember, not a word to Daphne. I rather hear what Savannah thinks first," Piper said.

"Sure thing," Renée replied.

Piper bolted up the stairs to do her hair and put on her makeup. She heard the door shut and realized Renée had left. While she was applying the finishing touches, her cell phone rang. She ran into the bedroom just in time to see "Babe" on the caller I.D. "Scott," she said as she rolled her eyes. She answered.

"Um, yeah. Hello, PJ, how are you?" Scott said.

"What do you care?" Piper replied.

"Look, I would like for us to remain cordial. It just didn't work out. And I thought it would be best to call and inform you that I filed for divorce. I got all I wanted out the house and I don't plan to try to get anything else. You can keep the house."

"Yeah, whatever." Piper clicked End Call. *I don't want to start my day like this. I have too much to do*, she thought. "Why, Scott?!" she yelled to no one. "Why?!"

She fell to the floor, pulled her knees to her chest, and cried. She had a nice long cry. She cried over Scott, she cried over her having cancer and she cried that no one was there to hold her, to ease the pain she felt gyrating through her heart. Her phone rang again. She assumed it was Scott and didn't bother to look.

After regaining her composure, she began her morning regimen over again. She removed the smeared make-up and applied her daily moisturizer. She heard the buzz of her cell, notifying her that she had a text message.

I guess Scott just finished his miniseries apology through a text message, Piper thought.

After getting dressed, she realized that it was not Scott who called, but Daphne. She checked her text messages next and realized Daphne had texted her instead of leaving a message. She grabbed her coat and headed downstairs, reading the text: *Hey PJ, my vacation starts today, would you like for me to go with you to your appointments? I have the time and I promise I will be dressed and ready to go when you get here. I hope you haven't left yet.*

"Great," Piper said sarcastically to herself. She debated during the walk to her car if she wanted to be bothered with Daphne or not. Having Daphne present could work to her advantage, as Daphne had been through this process before.

Once her phone was connected to her Lexus Bluetooth, she phoned Daphne. "Hi, Daphne, I would love for you to ride with me. I have to go to the Valley to tour the facility where I'm going to have the chemo treatments and have blood work done."

"Good. Come by and pick me up. I'll be ready. Pinky promise," Daphne said and hung up.

"Pinky promise?" Piper said as she disconnected her phone. She instantly realized that she couldn't recall Daphne sharing in the family fun of the pinky promises. "I guess I'm in for one heck of a day."

Chapter Four

Piper tried to listen to as much rap music as her ears could stand as she drove the freeway, headed to the California Hills Estates where Daphne and her family lived in a gated community. Daphne was not a fan. Piper hoped the music might prevent some unwanted conversations.

Henry, the gate attendant, waved Piper through. He knew every Jackson — they spent many holiday celebrations at Daphne's home. It was a minute's drive to the back of the sprawling community. When Piper turned the corner onto San Rafael Drive, she noticed a woman in a powder-blue sweat suit, with a white cross-body Guess purse and powder-blue tennis shoes. She looked familiar. She was speaking to one of Daphne's neighbors. Daphne did not do sportswear, so Piper shrugged off the thought of it being her. As she approached the driveway, she realized it was indeed Daphne. Looking like a high school cheerleader. Daphne hugged her neighbor and trotted to Piper's car.

"Good morning, Piper," she said, all smiles.

"Daphne! I thought you didn't wear sweat suits," Piper said.

"There comes a time in a woman's life when she decides to make a change, for the better."

Piper stared her up and down with her jaw dropped nearly to her chest. "I agree. So, what happened to you that was so drastic? Are you and Sherwin doing all right?" Piper asked.

"Sherwin and I are great!" Daphne replied.

"Well, you look great, Daphne! Oh, I have to call Harm!"

"Wait," Daphne said. "Let this day be just about you and I. I love my sister, and I love you, and this is a day I want to spend and share with you, okay?"

Looking a bit scared, Piper said, "Sure. But just to let you know, I am calling her later and telling her you wore a sweat suit." Piper backed her car from the driveway while staring Daphne up and down again.

"PJ, I thought this drive would be a good opportunity to talk to you about a few things. What exactly will you be having done today?"

"Well, Dr. Cheung wants me to have blood work completed. He's putting me on disability, so after my tour of the facility, I'll need to take the paperwork to my job."

"Good, the long drive will give us plenty of time to talk," Daphne said.

"Talk about what, exactly?" Piper asked.

"Piper, I've been here. I've been through what you are about to go through, and the easiest part of it is sitting and watching the medicine enter your veins. What you will see may be a shock to you."

"I'm a nurse. I've seen cancer patients before, and I've seen death before. Why would I be shocked?"

"It's who you will see when you go into the office. Patients are scheduled at all times, so they come and go. You will see people alone, and people with their friends and family. You will see them with hair, without hair. With good wigs and bad wigs. You are going to see people of all ages and different ethnicities. When I walked in the door for my first chemo treatment, my heart dropped. I saw women and men from the age of eighteen to eighty. Some will look sick and some will look normal. You may even overhear success stories about how they survived the first round or how the chemo had affected their lives. I just want to be there for you, if you need me. And if you have questions, just ask."

Piper pondered her sister's words. She never thought about others. People like her, with maybe the same problem — or worse. That hadn't crossed her mind. At that moment, she was grateful for Daphne's presence. "Thanks, Daphne, I never thought about what the atmosphere would be like."

"You're welcome," Daphne said. "PJ, you can talk to me about Scott, if you like. Have you heard from him?"

"Yes, he called and said he was sorry it didn't work between the two of us and that he was filing for divorce."

"Oh, PJ, I'm so sorry. Are you going to be all right?"

"I'll get over it. I'll be fine. It gets easier day by day."

"Great attitude to have. I'm very proud of you," Daphne said.

"Daphne, I have to ask. What has changed in your life recently? You never wore jeans, or sweats. I didn't know you even owned any."

Daphne looked away with the largest grin on her face. "PJ, if I share this, you can't tell anyone. Agree?"

"Pinky promise," Piper said.

"Savannah's expecting. I'm going to be a grandmother. Sherwin and I are delighted to welcome our first grandchild."

"That's wonderful. I'm happy for Savannah and Eric," Piper said, staring straight ahead through the windshield. "Congratulations!"

"PJ, are you all right?" Daphne looked at her sister. She was crying. She just hoped they were tears of joy.

Piper, wiping her eyes with the back of her jacket, said, "Yeah, I just never thought of my niece having children before me."

"She's not that much younger than you are. You have plenty of time to become a mother."

"That's not what Scott says," said Piper.

"What did he say?"

"He said my cancer genes is what caused me not to become pregnant."

"Don't believe that. If it was meant for you to conceive, you would have. It just wasn't meant to be. Maybe it's him. It's not always the woman's fault. And there are alternatives. You can adopt. Even if you don't remarry, the option is there."

"Thanks, Daphne. Scott was my first love and I never fathomed having children with anyone else or even dating anyone else. And I do want to be a mother one day. Do you think the chemo will prohibit me from conceiving naturally?"

"I'm not sure, but we can do the research and find out."

To break the tense conversation about Scott, Piper asked, "When's the baby due, Granny?" Piper chuckled.

"She just found out she was pregnant. I hope she has the gender reveal at the baby shower. Oh, my goodness, the baby shower!" Daphne said, scrambling for her phone. "I have to find a caterer, someone to host the shower… Oh, there's so much to be done. I was so excited when she told Sherwin and me that I forgot we have to plan the shower."

"Wait a minute, sis! You're turning a new leaf, so let me just put a little bug in your ear. True, this will be your first grandchild, but let Savannah and her friends plan the shower. You can offer your help and make some suggestions, but let them handle it. Times have change and they have co-ed baby showers now."

"Co-ed?" she shouted.

"Yes. It's just advice, but I think Savannah would appreciate it."

"I will. I'll step back. Am I that bad, PJ?" Daphne asked.

"You're not bad, but sometimes, you can be a bit much to handle."

"I just tried to set a positive example for you and Harmony."

"You did. We're great. But this is their time. Just stand back a little bit."

"Thanks, PJ."

"Now I understand why she and Eric are looking to purchase a home."

"Yes, I began looking for property in my comm..." Daphne began to say.

Piper gave her a sharp look and said, "I know you don't expect them to purchase a $700,000 home, do you?"

"I guess not. I should not have even given that any thought," Daphne said.

"No, you shouldn't. FYI, most men do not like living within a five-mile radius of their in-laws."

Daphne laughed. "I guess I'd better back away from the house hunting, too."

"They have to live in it. It should be their decision."

"You're right, PJ."

"Renée is their realtor. You know they were meeting this morning, right?"

Daphne replied with a somber, "No."

"I asked Renée to mention to them that I will be selling my home, and if they are interested, I will give them a good price."

"PJ, that's wonderful. Savannah loves your house. That would be perfect. But do you think it's too big? They're just starting out."

"I'll make it affordable. Scott said that I can have the house, so he won't be a problem."

Daphne leaned over and kissed her sister on the cheek. "You are really sweet, PJ."

"All right, don't get motherly on me. We're almost there."

Chapter Five

Piper pulled into the parking lot of a beautiful building complex that resembled a first-class resort. Valet parking was available for all that were visiting the center. Passenger vans with the name "The Cheryl Lincoln Research and Oncology Center" printed on both sides were parked outside the three-story parking garage.

Two tall men dressed in black slacks and white shirts with bow ties approached both sides of Piper's car.

"Hello, miss, may I help you out the car?" Daphne's doorman said.

"Hello, miss," the other said as he helped Piper out of the car. "May I have your name, please?

"Piper Jackson-Evans," she said.

He jotted her name on the bottom of the ticket and gave Piper the other half.

"Excuse me," Daphne said. "What's the cost of the valet?"

"It's complimentary. Everyone here is a VIP, ma'am," Piper's doorman said with a smile.

"Well, isn't that nice. Thank you," Daphne responded.

In the back of the center, a gated park with a playground area for children was surrounded by towering trees and a flower garden. A three-tier stone water fountain separated the parking lot and the front entrance.

"It's quiet out here," Daphne said as she took in her surroundings. There were no homes near the center, only a few stores and a gas station.

Nervous, Piper said, "Yeah. Quiet."

Daphne grabbed Piper's elbow as they made their way to the front entrance. Double automatic doors greeted them. The waiting area was adorned with modern living room furniture, with flat-screen televisions mounted on the walls. Beautiful vases sat on the foyer tables. Modern abstract art was displayed neatly on the walls.

As they approached the semicircular front counter, the receptionist greeted them with a pleasant, "Hello.

Welcome to The Cheryl Lincoln Research Center. How may I help you?"

Piper stepped forward and said, "I'm here for two reasons: to have my blood drawn and to tour the facility."

"May I have your name, please?"

"It's Piper Evans."

"Thank you, Mrs. or Ms. Evans?"

"You can just refer to me as Piper."

"I'm Shelia. I'll contact Dr. Cheung and let him know that you're here for the tour. He'll be handling the tour himself. Here's your paperwork. Please go to Room 143 down the hall on your right."

"Do I return to this area when I'm done?" Piper asked.

"Yes, and have a seat in the waiting area."

"Thank you."

Piper and Daphne walked down the long corridor. The walls had pictures of donors, with a little note of thank-you for their donation under their names. Some rooms had the names of the donors on plaques. When they arrived at the laboratory, they approached an elderly woman sitting behind the receptionist desk. She greeted them with a smile. She had a name badge that read, "Hi, my name is Melody. I'm a volunteer."

She looked at the computer monitor and said, "Hi, are you Piper?"

"Yes, I am."

"Enter curtain area number three to have your blood drawn, and your guest can have a seat in the waiting area."

"Thank you," Piper and Daphne said in unison.

Daphne witnessed patients coming and going as she waited for Piper to complete her lab work. Melody approached her and asked, "Would you like a bottle of water while you wait?"

"Yes, please. Thank you."

Melody returned with the water just as Piper drew back the curtain, a purple bandage wrapped around the crease of her left elbow.

"All done, PJ?" Daphne asked.

"Yes."

"Thank you again," Daphne said to Melody.

"You're welcome."

"I wish this place existed when I had my treatments," Daphne said. "Everyone is so friendly and the center is really nice. Doesn't resemble a hospital at all."

"Yes, they are. I feel comfortable here. You almost forget why you're here," Piper said.

They returned to the waiting area and were greeted by Dr. Cheung. "Hello, Piper, how are you? And who's this? Your mom?"

"No, she's my sister. Hello, Doctor," Piper said. She looked to Daphne to see if Dr. Cheung's statement had offended her, but she appeared to be fine.

"My apologies," Dr. Cheung said as he extended his hand to Daphne.

"It's an honest mistake. We're twenty-plus years apart," Daphne said as she shook the doctor's hand.

"Ready to tour the facility?" he asked.

"Yes," Piper said.

"I'll lead the way. If you have questions, please don't hesitate to interrupt me."

"Great," Daphne said.

"This is what we call the main floor lobby. The seating area is for guests of patients that don't want to sit and watch patients get their treatments. We try to make everyone that comes through those doors as comfortable as possible. You've been to the lab so no need to walk back down that corridor. Let's head in the opposite direction to the cafeteria. Here we have very healthy options — and some that are not so healthy. This cafeteria is for everyone. We have a staff lounge on the second floor along with private rooms for patients to relax prior to their treatments."

"Do you offer only chemo treatments?" Daphne asked.

"We do a lot of research. The second floor is where research studies are done as well. Testing new medications and medical procedures. Our goal is to try and cure cancer."

They headed to the elevators. "We're now going to the second floor," Dr. Cheung said.

They passed a few offices, two large conference rooms, and patient rooms. Some had the doors open so they could see what was inside. Those with the doors closed were occupied.

"There's a napping area and computer lounge for patients and their guests at the end of the hall. Many of the patients that are not transported here by our drivers have family and friends to bring them. Most have to take off work but want to be supportive and stay while the patients are having their treatments. Here, they can access the internet, do work, make phone calls. Across the hall is the napping area. We have patients that may be here for up to five hours, and we allow their guests to nap, if need be," Dr. Cheung explained.

"I met Melody downstairs. She's a volunteer, right? Are there many volunteers here at the center?" Piper asked.

"We have many. Most are former patients and some are people who just want to help out. They assist with the second floor mostly. The children's ward is on the fourth floor. I normally won't take patients to view that floor, unless they have a child going through treatments."

"That's considerate," Daphne said.

"I'll take you to the third floor next, where you will be having your treatments."

They exited the elevator on the third floor. It was a spacious, family-room–like atmosphere, with large flat-screens placed along the pastel walls, surrounded by living-room furniture and coffee tables with books and magazines.

"This is where you will come to have treatments. You will check in here, with these nurses. Once they call your name you will go in the back. There are patients currently having treatments there. Do you care to visit that area?"

"Yes, please," Piper said.

They entered the double doors and heard the sound of ocean waves softly in the background.

"This area is what we call the group area." There were several chairs that reclined, with smaller chairs for guests next to those having treatments.

"Down the hall this way is where we have private rooms, for those who wish to have their treatments in private," Dr. Cheung said. "The basement is another area we will not visit. It's for those who are receiving radiation. So, what do you think?" he asked.

"It's a really nice facility," Piper said.

"What's the cost for her to have her treatments here at this facility?" Daphne asked.

"What isn't covered by her medical insurance is covered by the donations we receive. No one has to pay an out-of-pocket cost."

"Doctor, how can you afford to run this facility? I'm not trying to be nosey, but the practicality of it — I know it cost a fortune to run," Daphne said.

"Theodore Lincoln donated millions to establish this center in his wife, Cheryl's, name. She died of complications from breast cancer. She would tell him when having her treatments what would have made her more comfortable during her visits to the hospital. She wanted an atmosphere that did not resemble a hospital. The valet was her idea, as well as having home furnishings instead of hospital decor."

"It's really beautiful. Do you believe this is the most viable option for me and my case?" Piper asked.

Having exploratory surgery is a risk. I believe starting you out on Chemotherapy is the best solution."

"Great! When do we begin?"

Chapter Six

It had been a long day. Piper was exhausted. After dropping Daphne off, she went home to relax. She read over the paperwork she was given regarding the medications she would receive and their potential side effects. Docetaxel was the drug listed at the top of the page. One common side effect for cancer patients was hair loss.

What will I do if I lose my hair? Piper thought. She read the whole list of side effects: hair loss, nausea, vomiting, weakness, missed menstrual periods, and fingernail or toenail changes. She looked down at her beautifully manicured hands and pedicured toes. "Hopefully, they'll have something to protect my nails."

Vomiting was one thing she did not like to do at all. She read that there was medication that should prevent nausea while she received her treatments. She would definitely focus on getting it.

She wondered if she would get all or just some of the side effects. While she continued to read, her phone rang. "Not Scott!" she said aloud.

"Hello, Piper, how did your day go?" Harmony asked.

"It went well, Harm. The facility is really nice. Daphne went with me," Piper said.

"How did that go?" Harmony asked.

"Surprisingly well. Harm, she wore sweats," Piper said.

"What??" Harmony shouted.

"I know, right! We had a really long talk, and she was very helpful. Not motherly. She warned me about what I was about to walk into, and it's prepared me mentally," Piper said.

"WHAT?!" Harmony shouted again, even louder. "She wore sweats? I've never seen Daphne in anything but a dress, skirt or slacks in all my twenty-four years on this earth. What!"

"She's different and for a good cause."

"Sherwin left?" Harmony chuckled.

"That's not a good cause, Harm. I promised not to tell. Pinky promised."

"WHAT! She did the pinky promise? She's never done that."

"I know. She's different, Harm, but I don't know how long it will last."

"I hate I missed all the fun, PJ. How are you feeling?"

"I'm fine. I'm going over to Mom and Dad's for dinner. I told Mom I would join them and tell them about the facility."

"Jason and I are going out to dinner with his brothers. It's like a triple date."

"Dinner and a movie?" Piper asked

"Dinner and a movie," Harmony replied.

"Well, we will get together soon. Talk to you later, Harm."

"See ya!"

After her conversation with Harmony, Piper's phoned buzzed. A group text was coming through. Family alert. It was from Daphne and read: *Dinner, this Sunday, May 16th, 6:00 pm. All family invited. Sherwin and Daphne's place. Big Announcement!*

Piper read the text and knew the big announcement was for Savannah and Eric's new arrival. Back-to-back buzzing meant family members were responding. Brothers and their wives and their children, accepting the invite.

I guess everyone will be there. Might as well make my announcements as well. I'll make mine first. That way, it won't be a totally somber day.

Piper texted Daphne in a private message to get the okay. *Bad news first?*

Daphne: *Of course.*

Piper continued her reading. She had to be well-versed to discuss this with her parents. Being educators, both Mr. and Mrs. Jackson expected their children to read and be prepared to answer questions, to do their research before approaching them.

"Alcohol should not be consumed during chemo. Although it may not affect the drug you're taking, it may have an effect on other drugs that you may have to take. To be safe, do not consume alcohol," Piper read aloud. "Well, I might as well crack open this bottle of Chardonnay." Piper was opening the bottle when the doorbell rang.

"Who is it?" she asked.

"It's me, Scott."

The wine glass suddenly slipped from her left hand and she caught it before it hit the floor with her right. She didn't know who would be visiting her, and her last thought was Scott.

"Hang on," she said.

Piper set the glass of wine on the kitchen counter. She got a dish towel and tried to dry the wine that had spilled onto her shirt.

"Piper?" Scott said through the closed door.

Piper opened the wood door, ready to be one hundred percent sarcastic. "How may I help you, sir?" she asked.

"PJ, can I come in?"

"Got rid of your key already?"

"No, I just thought it would be inappropriate for me to use it, and I'm not staying here."

"Yeah, whatever." She opened the door wider so that Scott could enter. In his hand, he held a large manila envelope. "Is that what I think it is? If so, just leave it on the counter and I'll get to it," Piper said.

"PJ, I want to talk to you."

"About what, Scott? I think you said it all. You left me and said you wanted a divorce. What else could there possibly be for you to say?" Piper said angrily. "And it look like you wasted no time in having your father draw up the papers for our divorce." She snatched the envelope from his hand and threw it in the kitchen, where it landed on the floor.

"You don't have to be that way, PJ. My father thought it was best to just get it over with. Since we were married in

Las Vegas, it won't take that long. He's going to handle everything. And he thinks it's in our best interest to sell this house," Scott said.

"OUR best interest? You said I could have the house. My parents gave us the money to purchase this house!" Piper shouted.

"It was a fixer-upper, remember. It wasn't all together," Scott said.

"Yeah, I remember. Getting a fixer was my idea. Every floor, wall, and nail in this place was my decision. You were too busy working, putting in late hours at the firm to deal with it, and now you want me to sell it and give you half?"

"It's considered community property in a divorce in California."

"You sound like a textbook. Did your daddy tell you that, too? You took the entertainment center and TVs. What about that?"

"I didn't think you wanted them. You spent more time in your office than watching TV," Scott said.

"You didn't bother to ask either. You just took what you wanted and left. Get out, Scott. GET OUT!" Piper pointed to the front door.

"Just let me know when you sign the paperwork," Scott said as he left.

Piper slammed the door behind him, hard enough to rattle the house a little. Returning to her much-needed drink, she took the wine glass and gulped the contents, then retreated to her sanctuary, bottle of wine in hand. She needed a long bath before heading out to her parents' home for dinner.

She stood in the mirror and looked over her body. It was not flawed. It did not look sick. It didn't look like cancer. It was what God intended for her to have.

After her bath, Piper realized that she may have had a little too much wine, and thought it might be better if she didn't drive. She called Brock Jr. to see what his plans were, to see if he could take her to her parents' and stay with her.

She considered calling his house phone, but decided against it. His wife, Ashlyn, would want to talk to her for hours on end. She dialed the cell, and he answered on the first ring. "Hey PJ. What's up?"

"Hey, big brother. Are you busy?"

"Not really. What's going on?"

"I'm supposed to go to Mommy and Daddy's house for dinner to let them know my chemo schedule and to tell them about the facility, and I think I need a ride," she said.

"Sure, I'll come by and pick you up. What's wrong with your car?" Brock Jr. asked.

"Nothing. Just had a little too much wine."

"I'm on the way."

Brock Jr. arrived shortly thereafter. Knowing Scott was no longer living in the house, he used his key to let himself in. "PJ? I'm here," he yelled.

"Be there in a sec," she yelled back.

Piper stood at the top of the staircase and stared down, wondering how she was going to manage her descent.

"PJ? How much did you have to drink?" Brock Jr. asked as he headed up the stairs.

"Well, I found out that I won't be able to drink once I begin treatment, so I decided to finish the bottle I had in the cooler." She took one step down and stumbled into Brock Jr.'s arms.

"I'll call Mom and Dad and let them know you'll be by tomorrow."

"No, I'm good, Brock. I'll be fine."

"Dad would not approve and you know it. Tomorrow will be a better day."

Brock Jr. picked his little sister up and took her to her bedroom. He laid her across the bed. Piper was not drunk, only "intoxicated mildly," as she put it.

"Hey Dad. I'm at PJ's. I have a project for her to assist me with. Do you mind if she comes by tomorrow for dinner?" Brock Jr. asked his dad.

"Put her on the phone," Mr. Jackson said.

Brock Jr. handed Piper the phone. "Sit up," he whispered to her.

"Hey Daddy, I don't feel too good. Will it be all right if I come by tomorrow for dinner?" PJ asked.

"What's the problem?"

Piper knew she could never get away with telling her father an untruth. "I drank a little too much wine."

"Piper, you knew we were expecting you for dinner. Why would you indulge in an excessive amount of wine? What transpired today that made you want to drink as much as you did?"

"Scott came by and served me with divorce papers. Daddy, when he called the other day, he said I could have the house. He said he didn't want it," Piper cried.

"I see. I will speak with you tomorrow. Hand the phone to Brock," her father said.

"Bye, Daddy." She did as she was told and gave Brock Jr. the phone.

"Yes, sir?" Brock Jr. said.

"I want you to speak with Scott. Let him know he will not take advantage of my daughter, even if he does have a high-power attorney for a father."

"Yes, sir." Brock replied.

"Find out what happened and report back to me. And Brock?"

"Yes, sir?"

"Don't discuss your findings with Piper. I'll take care of that."

"Got it. I'll take care of that tomorrow. Goodnight, Dad," Brock Jr. said.

He hung up and looked at Piper, who was staring him in the face. "So, what were all the 'yes sirs' about? What does he want you to do?"

"Speak to Scott. He wants me to make sure he knows that we're not going to let him hurt you anymore."

"Brock, I don't think anyone could ever hurt me anymore. What's wrong with me? Why did he leave me, Brock? Why?" Piper cried.

Brock Jr. held his sister and said, "I don't know why he left, PJ, but it wasn't because of you." He grabbed her gently by the chin and looked deeply into her eyes. He could read her soul and all the pain she was in. With all sincerity, he said, "You are beautiful, in and out, and if you ask me, he didn't deserve you. Don't worry, after I speak with him, he'll never hurt you again. Pinky promise."

Chapter Seven

My timing was just bad. Piper know I would not intentionally hurt her. The cancer was a surprise. I didn't expect that. Maybe she doesn't have cancer. Maybe she just wanted my sympathy because she knows. Does she? Does she know everything? Oh, man. How could she have found out? No one knows. I've been very careful for over a year and have never been discovered. I was very careful not to put her in Piper's circle. And she had no reason to look. She knew the half-truth, which was satisfying to her. She enjoyed being Piper's successor, or so she thought. I just never thought it mattered if I was married or not.

As he drove, Scott tried to justify his actions. He knew there was no excuse for him to have treated her the way he did. Now that he was living away from Piper and with someone else, no one would judge him. "We are getting a divorce," he could say to anyone who had curious eyes or questioned him.

Now I can live my life the way I want to live my life. I'm not ashamed to take her out, locally now. He smiled to himself. *We will be happy, just the three of us. For so long, I wanted this type of relationship with Piper, but it never happened. We planned and tried, tried and planned, and nothing. With her, we didn't try. Just one drunken night and, low and behold, nine months later, a son. My very own son. So that means I was meant to be with Darla, and not Piper. Piper couldn't give me a child. I do love her, though. I hope she's lying about the cancer. Why, though? Why lie? After what her family went through with Daphne and her bout with cancer. She wouldn't do that to me: make me feel ashamed for leaving her. She's joking. She doesn't have cancer. She just wanted me to stay.*

Walking through the front door, anticipating the smiles and giggles from his son, was the greatest feeling Scott had ever experienced.

Darla, in her yoga pose, sat next to the carrier that held their five-month-old bouncing baby boy. He was a handsome, younger image of Scott. Slick, black hair dangling down the back of his neck.

Darla was exquisite. The perfect image of the woman he always wanted to marry.

"Hello, darling," he said as he walked toward her and kissed her on the cheek. "Hello, son." He lifted him from the carrier to raise him above his head and back again.

"I wouldn't do that if I were you. He just ate," Darla explained.

"Do you think your mom can babysit? I want to take you to dinner, just you and I," Scott asked.

"I'm sure I can twist her arm!" Darla said, smiling. "What's the occasion?"

"I feel like seafood. Jacob's by the Pier. I have my heart set on going. Go, get started. Make your calls and I'll change," Scott said.

"What's with you, Scott? I've never seen you like this."

"Our life is about to change, for the better!" he said.

Darla didn't want to ask. She wanted the element of surprise, but she suspected a proposal was going to happen tonight. He was taking her to their favorite place and he was in a good mood, which was different.

"Are we celebrating a partnership with the firm?" she yelled from the bedroom.

"That will come in time," Scott yelled from the living room.

Darla became giddy at the thought of it being a proposal. She jumped and laughed. She had always wanted to marry Scott. Since the day she met him in the club, it had been a done deal, as far as she was concerned.

As long as he didn't come with baggage, they would be the perfect couple. She thought Scott's living with his sister to help rear her children was so unselfish of him. He was perfect. Having to raise three children on her own was too much for his sister to handle. Scott stepped up to help.

We are finally going to begin living our life the way we talked about. Just him, the little one, and me. I have so much to plan. I better wait for the ring before I begin the guest list, Darla thought.

The drive to the restaurant was full of laughter and talking. Mostly, Darla trying to get something out of Scott.

Once seated, they ordered wine to celebrate.

"What is it, Scott? I've waited all this time and you haven't mentioned anything."

"My sister has decided to sell her house and give me a large sum. Now we can get out of your dad's condo and begin looking for our own home. What do you think?" Scott said.

Darla felt empty. She just knew she was getting a ring. Scott noticed the sorrowful look on her face. He didn't like it.

"Darla, I thought this was great news. We are finally going to have enough money to buy our own home."

"Don't you think we should get married first, Scott?" she asked.

Scott couldn't say what he wanted to say: that he was not completely out of his marriage with Piper. Darla didn't know about the marriage, so he had to think of a clever way to explain why it was not wise for them to get married right now. He still loved Piper and hadn't totally gotten her out of his system.

"We'll talk marriage later. Let's eat."

They ate in awkward silence. No one said a word.

After dinner, they stayed for a while to listen to the band that was playing instead of rushing home.

03&0

Brock Jr. went home after Piper fell asleep. His home life was not at its highest peak. He would be fifty next year and had been contemplating a major change in his life. He had not fallen out of love with his wife, Ashlyn. They were just not on the same page these days. His son, William, was away at school in Washington, DC. His daughter, Brittany, was entering her second year of college in New York, and Brock felt like being a teenager again. Going skating and going to dances, hanging with friends and going for nightly rides. Ashlyn felt she'd lived that phase of her life and felt they should be anticipating marrying their children off and waiting on grandchildren.

It was a Friday night. It was only nine o'clock, and Ashlyn didn't have work in the morning, but she was already fast asleep. Brock Jr. shook his head and went to the den to catch the scores for Major Baseball League. His concentration waned. He couldn't help but think how they could be out skating or taking a drive down the coast.

He went to wake up Ashlyn and ask her to go for a drive. He tip-toed into the dark room and snuggled up behind her. She reached her hand back and wrapped her arm around his back.

"You're back? How's Piper? Did everything go all right with your parents?"

"Baby, let's take a drive and I'll tell you all about it."

"Oh, honey. It's late," Ashlyn said.

"It's only nine o'clock and it's Friday. I'm off tomorrow and you're off tomorrow." He snuggled a little closer and put his nose in a crease of her neck to inhale her scent. His wife's scent was the sweetest, the freshest he had ever smelled. No one ever smelled as sweet as his wife. He nibbled on her neck, trying to convince her to get up and take a ride.

"Not tonight, honey. I'm tired. I have to do shopping tomorrow and send the kids care packages in the morning."

"Ash, baby, you know I love the kids. They're away at school. Can I get some time with you?"

"We spend every night together. What is it that you want from me? What's going on with you, Brock? We go through this every weekend."

"When we were younger, we would go somewhere every weekend."

"We were also in our teens and early twenties, Brock. You're having a midlife crisis. It will pass. Now, come to bed, honey."

"I'm not sleepy. I'll be back," he said.

"Where are you going?" Ashlyn sat up in their Cal King bed.

"For a ride."

"Be careful, honey, and don't stay out too late." Ashlyn laid her head on her pillow to go back to sleep.

Brock Jr. was not happy. He entered the garage through the kitchen and thought about getting on the Harley. He opted for the Cadillac. He felt like cruising. He searched the garage for his music CDs. He popped one into the CD player as he opened the garage with the electronic opener. Back in the day, he would have cruised down Crenshaw, but that scene had long since passed.

He was immersed in his music and didn't notice the forty-five-minute drive to the pier. Realizing he hadn't eaten, he decided to visit Jacob's for takeout. The hostess offered him a seat.

"Not tonight. Can I get something to go?" he asked her.

"Sure, here's a menu. Have a seat at the bar and I'll return shortly to take your order."

As he read the menu, trying to get his brain and stomach to agree on a meal, he overheard a couple talking. He turned to see Scott having a conversation with an attractive woman with a model's figure.

"Well, just the man I need to see," Brock Jr. said.

Knowing the voice all too well, Scott turned abruptly to make sure Brock Jr. was alone and didn't have the whole Jackson clan with him. He often told Piper her family traveled in packs. It was not unusual to see the entire clan at one event or at the smallest occasion. Her family supported each other's causes, from the patriarch, Mr. Jackson, to his youngest grandchild.

"Hey, Brock, how are you?" he said. Scott stepped over to Brock Jr.'s imposing six-foot, five-inch frame and shook his hand. He always felt like Tattoo from *Fantasy Island* when he stood in the room with the Jackson men.

"Things are good," Brock Jr. said. "And you are, beautiful?" he said as he extended his hand.

"I'm Darla," she said, shaking his hand.

"Hm, Darla, this is PJ's brother, Brock," said Scott.

"Pleasure to meet you, Brock. How's PJ doing? I hope she's well," she said with sincerity.

Looking directly down at Scott, smile vanquished, Brock Jr. said, "PJ's good." Returning his gaze to Darla, he said, "Did you guys go to school together?"

"No, I've never met her. Only heard about her. Good things," she said.

"Good things, huh?" Brock Jr. said.

"Yes. Scott told me about his past relationships."

"Is that right." Brock Jr. said and returned his focus to Scott.

"It's really nice seeing you, Brock. Give my best to the family," Scott said and tried to walk away.

Brock Jr. grabbed his shoulder and gently guided him back around to look him in the eyes. Sort of.

"Scott, can we get together tomorrow? Meet me at the gym. Let's work out, for old time's sake."

"Hm, sure. Usual time?" Scott asked as he prepared to leave.

"Yeah, usual time," Brock Jr. said. "It was nice meeting you — Darla, is it?"

"Yes, Darla. And it was really nice meeting you as well." She and Scott walked off.

Brock Jr. placed his order, called Ashlyn from his cell to let her know that he was en route, and asked if she wanted some dessert. He informed her that something really interesting had just transpired and he needed her awake and focused when he arrived.

The hostess returned with Brock Jr.'s order and he started home. He hadn't been in a rush to get home to Ashlyn in a long while. The incident reminded him of why he married her in the first place. She was his best friend, his confidante. The woman who had borne his beautiful children.

He arrived home overly excited. He wanted to hold and kiss his wife and tell her what he witnessed by happenstance.

"Baby, I need you to get up. I have something to tell you."

"Now, Brock?"

"It's important, Ash."

"Okay, let me wash my face, and you will have my undivided attention."

When she returned, Brock Jr. was devouring his crab legs and shrimp scampi. "Oh, honey, that looks good. Can I have a taste?" she asked.

Brock Jr. handed Ashlyn the plate and told her what had happened at PJ's, how she was too intoxicated to go to their parents'. Brock also mentioned how upset Piper was that Scott had left. "She thinks it was her fault. He served her with divorce papers today and she didn't take it too well.

Dad wants me to speak to him, to find out what's really going on, and I saw him tonight at Jacob's," he explained.

"Really? What a co-winkie-dink," she said.

"Not coincidental. I believe it was meant for me to see him. You know that saying? 'What's done in the dark shall come to light?' Well, the sun couldn't be any brighter than it was tonight. He was on a date."

"A date? Didn't he just leave a couple of weeks ago?"

"Right. She thinks Piper is just his past girlfriend."

"Wait, how did you guys get on the subject of Piper? Brock, what did you do, honey?"

"Not me. Scott introduced me as Piper's brother, and the woman asked how she was doing. I asked if she knew Piper from school and she said Scott told her about all his high school girlfriends," Brock Jr. said.

"All? Wasn't Piper the first? At least, she thinks she was the first. Oh, honey, you can't tell her. It would crush her. At least, not now," Ashlyn stated.

"I know. I have to tell my dad. I can't lie to him. I have to tell him. I'm meeting Scott tomorrow at the gym for a workout. I'll go see Dad afterwards."

"Brock, if he's dating this soon, I'm sure it wasn't their first date."

"Yeah, I know. And something tells me it's something more serious than any of us ever suspected."

Chapter Eight

Just as Brock Jr. expected, Scott was a no-show at the gym. He didn't want to feel as if his time was wasted, so he put in a much-needed workout, anyway. After his workout, he tried to call Scott once again. No answer. "Figures," he said and called his dad. "Hey Dad, you got a minute?"

"Sure, son." Mr. Jackson said.

"I ran into Scott last night while getting dinner."

"Really!"

"Yes. Um, Dad, he wasn't alone."

"I see. Do you know her?" Mr. Jackson asked.

Looking at the phone, Brock thought to himself, *This man has ESP!*

"No, sir. I don't. But it appears she knows about Piper. Just what, I don't know."

"Has Piper discussed any other details about the breakup with you?" his father asked.

"Only that he filed papers and want half of the house."

"Thanks, son. Don't disclose this conversation with anyone. I'll handle if from here," Mr. Jackson said.

"But, Dad, I really didn't get a chance to talk to Scott alone," Brock Jr. explained.

"I'll handle it," Mr. Jackson said.

"Yes, sir," Brock Jr. said. "I'll stop by soon. Tell Mom I said hello!"

Mr. Jackson hung up the phone without responding.

☙❧

Piper woke up exhausted. Eager to get the day over, she invited her parents to lunch at her home instead of having a late dinner. As she prepared for their arrival, she made sure she had her treatment plan together.

Her father arrived, alone. "Where's Mom?" she asked.

"She went to help Daphne prepare for this weekend." Her father kissed her on the cheek. "It will be just you and I today. Now, before we get started on our lunch, let's have a sit-down. How are things going with you and Scott? It's apparent he's not returning."

"No, he's not."

"How long has this been going on, Piper? Have you guys been having financial difficulties lately?"

"No, not financial. He's not happy that I haven't been able to get pregnant. We've been trying for the last three years, and nothing. He won't get tested and my results are inconclusive."

"So, what you are saying is he wants a divorce because you can't have children. When did he first ask for the divorce? I'm only concerned about you now. Not you and Scott. Your health and well-being is my main concern. I want you to know that no matter what happens, I'm here for you and will protect you and help you get whatever it is that you need to get through this ordeal. Do you understand?"

"Yes, Daddy. I do."

"Did he ask for the divorce a while ago or just recently?" her father asked.

"Daddy, I was shocked and hurt. I told him my cancer situation and he said he didn't want to deal with it. Basically."

Mr. Jackson clasped his large hands together in a manner that frightened Piper.

"So, he's never mention divorce before that?" he asked.

"No, Daddy. Lately, he hadn't been getting in until late. Working with his dad on several projects at the law firm. He called the other day and said he was filing for divorce and that I can have the house, but according to the papers his father drew up, he wants half the house. I don't think it's fair that he leaves me and I get the short end of the stick and he gets everything he wants. It's not fair."

Her father took a look around the house. He noticed it was the same as the night he first came by to see about his daughter. "Piper, this house and everything in it is materialistic. You can get another house. You can replace what he took. As your father, what would you like for me to do?"

In the most babyish voice she could muster up, she said, "Let Brock beat him up?"

Her father gave her a look that meant her request did not deserve a response.

"Nothing, Daddy, I'll be fine," she said, changing her tone.

"Now, are you going to sell the house? Let him have half. Right now, your health should be your main concern. Stress is not good for you."

"But it's not fair. He left here with everything, including my heart. I can't get half of that back."

Feeling the pain in his daughter's voice, he knew he could not tell her what Brock Jr. saw last night. It just might kill her.

"Come here, baby girl." He held out his arms for her to fall into a huge hug. "Maybe Scott was not the person for you. He's not the only man left in this world. There are many men available. But that's something you shouldn't concern yourself with at this time. Let's have a look at your treatment schedule."

Piper retrieved the brochure and the paperwork, handed them to her father, and left to prepare lunch.

Mr. Jackson read through the brochure and the information about her medication, mainly the side effects. He suggested that he be the one to take her for her first visit.

"Piper, I think you need to come and stay with us, at least for a while. So that we can see how this medication will affect you."

"I'll think about it, Dad."

"What is there to think about?" he said.

"I don't want to be that child that has to move back with her parents because times are hard."

"Times are hard and you need the help. Can you afford to pay the mortgage on this house?"

She hadn't thought about that. Scott mentioned the divorce out of the blue and she never thought about how she would survive, being on a leave of absence and having to manage the household alone.

"Savannah is looking to purchase a home, she and Eric. Maybe Renée can work something out. It may be possible to rent them the house until they're approved to buy," Piper said.

"If Savanna and Eric want to buy your house, I will help them."

"Daddy, are you this undercover rich guy?" she laughed.

Mr. Jackson chuckled and said, "No, just a smart guy. I knew from the day each of you were conceived that you would need financial help, and I put myself in a position to do just that. And stay of out my pockets," he laughed.

"Oh, Daddy, I don't know what I would do without you," Piper said as she put her arms around him.

"Nor I, you," he said in return. "Is lunch ready?" He felt his eyes beginning to tear.

"Let's eat!" Piper said with enthusiasm.

They chatted about the facility. Piper mentioned all the perks of the institute. She mentioned the computer room, told her dad about the different options she had.

"Sounds good, Piper," her dad said.

He finished his lunch and left. During his drive home he contemplated calling Scott, to give him a piece of his mind, but he thought it might not be wise. He decided to wait until Piper was well, done with chemo, to let her know what a deadbeat Scott was in the first place. His number-one priority, for now, was Piper.

Chapter Nine

Piper had not noticed before how quiet the mornings in her home had become since Scott left. The hollow sound disturbed her.

Savannah should be happy here, Piper thought as she reached for her cell.

Quick to answer the phone for her Aunt Piper, Savannah said a very cheery, "Hello, Auntie PJ? How are you?"

"I'm well, Vanna." Piper's nickname for her niece. "How are you and Eric doing?" she asked.

"We're great, Auntie. How are you feeling? Mom said you are a bit under the weather."

"I'll be fine, Savannah. Did Renée mention that I'll be putting the house up for sale?"

"Yes, she did. Eric loves your house, and I like it as well, but I don't think we can afford a home as large as yours."

"Can you and Eric stop by before going to your mother's house? Then we can talk over a few things."

"Mom wants us to arrive early so we can go over the announcements. Can we meet there instead?" Savannah said.

"Sure. I'll meet you guys in the gazebo."

"See you then, Auntie."

"See ya," Piper said.

The Jacksons began arriving at the home of Sherwin and Daphne Montgomery. The guard waved them in, one by one, as they approached the gate. The house was full of family by the time Piper arrived. Everyone was anxious to hear the announcement.

The party was held in the backyard. Behind the pool was a covered gazebo. In it, a fire pit surrounded by peach-colored lounge chairs. On the opposite side of the yard stood many family members enjoying drinks at the outdoor bar. Some were in swimsuits, relaxing by the pool or sitting in the Jacuzzi. The men mostly hung out in the den, playing dominoes. The DJ played smooth jazz as everyone socialized.

Piper headed to the gazebo to meet Savannah and Eric but was caught off-guard by Savannah's in-laws. "Hello, PJ, how are you?" Mr. and Mrs. McDaniel's said.

"I'm well. And how have you been?" Piper said as she hugged them both.

"We're great." They looked around. "Where's Scott? Is he indoors?"

"Um, no, he's not attending today's function," Piper replied. She made her excuses and continued to the gazebo. Eric and Savannah were sitting in the lounge chair, admiring Savannah's stomach, when Piper arrived.

"Hello, Auntie," Savannah said.

"Hey PJ," Eric said as he stood and gave her a hug.

"Hey guys. Your mom told me you were expecting. Congratulations. She only told me. No one else," Piper explained.

"Well, that's okay, Auntie. How are you feeling?" Savannah asked.

"Good. I have a few things to tell you. Just promise you won't get emotional, please," Piper said.

With a worried look on her face, Savannah said, "Okay, pinky promise."

"I have a battle ahead of me. Actually, a couple of battles. I have breast cancer, and Scott and I are no longer together."

Savannah stood on her feet and hugged Piper. When she was done, Eric hugged her as well.

"What are the plans for treating the cancer?" Eric asked.

"I'll begin chemotherapy soon," she said.

"Great, the sooner the better. Mom survived and you can, too, Auntie PJ," Savannah said.

"I know, honey, and I will," Piper said.

"If you need anything, PJ, all you have to do is ask," Eric said.

"There is one thing. Since Scott and I are getting a divorce, if you guys are serious about buying the house, it's yours."

"PJ, I'm not sure if we would even qualify to purchase your home. It would be nice. I really love your home," Eric said.

"Well, you do have a couple of options. Dad wants me to move in with them, so that they can get me to my chemo sessions, and I will stay at their place while I'm recuperating. So, if you're interested in renting first, we can work something out."

"Really?" Eric said with excitement.

"Really. I need the help, as well as the two of you," Piper said.

"Are you sure, Auntie? We don't have enough furniture in our one-bedroom apartment to fill up that house," Savannah said.

"I will throw in the furniture as well. I can't take it with me, so I might as well include it in the sale."

Eric smiled and felt grateful. "My parents will be willing to help with furniture as well. Let's do it, babe. I really love that house," Eric said.

"Well, there's a lot to consider. The monthly payments, for one. How much we will need to budget for bills. That sort of thing," Savannah said.

The noise of a spoon tapping a glass interrupted their conversation. A voice over the speaker said, "Piper, Savannah, and Eric, please come to the DJ booth."

"That's our cue," Piper said. "And don't worry. If you guys want the house, it's yours."

"Thank you, Auntie," Savannah said.

"Thank you, PJ. You've given us a lot to consider," Eric said.

"Let's go and make our announcements," Piper said as she led the way to the DJ booth.

Mr. Jackson was standing there, talking to the DJ. "May I have your attention?" Mr. Jackson said sternly. As the murmurs subsided, he spoke. "We are gathered here today to celebrate family. Family is the bond that keep us all together. Before the announcements take place, I want everyone to know that this will be a happy occasion. No matter what is said, we are a strong family, with strong beliefs, and together we will stand tall and strong." Then he prayed: "Heavenly Father, we thank you for allowing us to gather as family today. Please continue to bless this family, those present and those that are far away. And Lord, please keep us close. Amen."

The crowd responded, "Amen."

He handed the mic to Piper and began to walk off when he felt Piper grab his arm. He remained by her side.

"Hello, family," she said. "Well there's no other way to do this but to say it. I have a battle ahead of me. I have cancer. I will begin treatment next week. I would like you all to pray for me and not feel sorry for me. I will beat this."

And the backyard erupted in applause. Harmony and Daphne stood side-by-side. Her brothers trotted up to stand next to Piper and said, "Job well done."

Some, like her nieces and small cousins, were crying. Her aunts and uncles, aware of her condition, gave her hugs and kisses.

Piper gave the mic to Eric so that he could make their big announcement. Sherwin, Daphne, and Mr. and Mrs. McDaniel stood next to their children.

Harmony, now standing and holding Piper's hand, said, "Well, I guess everyone knows what this announcement is about."

"Yeah, the rabbit died!" Piper said.

"Whose rabbit died?" Harmony's boyfriend, Jason, said as he and his two brothers walked up behind Harmony and Piper.

"It's a metaphor," Harmony said.

"Oh. Hey PJ," Jason said.

"Hello, PJ," echoed his brothers.

"Hi, guys," Piper said, half smiling.

"Hello, family," Eric said. "Savannah and I, along with our parents, would like to announce that we are expecting our first child."

The backyard erupted in cheers and congratulations.

Mr. Jackson returned to the DJ booth and said, "This family is getting larger by the moment. Congratulations, you two. My oldest grandchild is having my first great-grandchild. I couldn't be happier."

Everyone applauded.

"Eric, Savannah, let me pull you away from this crowd for a moment," Mr. Jackson said. "Are the two of you interested in purchasing Piper's home?"

"Granddaddy, we just spoke about it today. I'm not sure we can afford it," Savannah said.

"Yes, Mr. Jackson, it's a beautiful home and we would love to raise our family there, but we would have to work out the budget first."

"You guys have blessed me with my first great-grandchild. I'm beyond excited. I never thought of seeing another generation of Jacksons, but the two of you have made that possible. If you want the home, I will help you purchase it. We'll get together with Renée and figure out how this can be done," Mr. Jackson said.

With tears in his eyes, Eric ran to Mr. Jackson and shook his hand and said, "Thank you, Mr. Jackson. That is very kind of you."

"Happy to help!" Mr. Jackson said. He looked at his granddaughter. She looked somber. "What's the matter, Savannah? You don't want me to help you?" he asked.

"No, Granddaddy, it's not that. It's Auntie. She's sick, lost her husband, and now her home? It just doesn't feel fair to her."

"I want you guys to have it," Piper said as she walked up toward the end of Savannah's conversation.

"Oh, Auntie, I love you so much. I will take care of your home. I promise."

"Pinky promise?" Piper said as she stuck out her pinky.

"Pinky promise," Savannah said.

"Pinky promise," Eric said.

"Piper, will you ever outgrow pinky promises?" Mr. Jackson asked. And the gathering shared a group hug.

The DJ played rhythm and blues music as the partiers partied on the makeshift dance floor that Sherwin had built. "Let's Get Married" played, and Jason's brothers sang and danced along.

As Jason and Harmony danced, his brothers surrounded them. The three of them performed a routine in front of Harmony. She had no idea what was about to happen. She was used to the three of them clowning around when they were together. Everyone exited the dance floor, except for Jason and Harmony. Mr. Jackson walked up to Jason with a velvet box in his hand as the music was lowered to barely a whisper. Jason bent down on one knee. Harmony's smile changed to an expression of utter shock.

Jason opened the box and said, "Harmony, we have been together for three years now. I love you and, with your father's permission, I would like to have you as my wife."

Harmony looked from Jason to her father, to the family that stood watching. She was in tears.

"You have my permission," Mr. Jackson said.

"Ours, too!" said Brock Jr. and Davon.

"Harmony, will you marry me?" Jason asked.

"Yes, yes, yes. I'll marry you," Harmony cried.

"The last one. Jason, you have made me a very happy man," Mr. Jackson said.

"Oh, Daddy. You're going to miss me when I'm married."

As Mr. Jackson and Harmony hugged, he whispered in her ear, "Wanna bet! I'm having a great-grandbaby."

Chapter Ten

As the party continued, Piper's somber mood grew. She felt her news put a damper on the party and she was ready to leave. Despite the laughter and dancing surrounding her, she was not in the partying mood. Harmony noticed her sadness and excused herself from her fiancé.

"Hey PJ. Are you all right?" Harmony asked.

"I'll be fine. Congratulations on the engagement. Now that I'm no longer married, will I be a maid or matron of honor?" Piper asked, curious.

"Whichever title you want. This caught me by surprise. I had no idea he was going to propose. We talked about marriage, but I didn't think that it would be any time soon."

"Let me see that ring," Piper said.

Harmony held out her left hand and showed off the princess-cut, two-carat diamond solitaire ring. "We have a lot of planning to do, sis! I'm thinking about a yearlong engagement, at least."

Piper tilted her head and asked, "Why a year? Harmony, please don't consider me and my illness when planning your wedding. Please."

"We are like two peas in a pod. My wedding is nothing without you. You have to be a part of this celebration. I just want to make sure you're up to it."

"I promise, no matter how I'm feeling, I will make your wedding."

"Pinky promise?"

"Yeah, pinky promise," Piper said. "I think I'm going to sneak out and go home. I'm a little drained."

"Call me tomorrow, PJ."

"Will do!" she said and left the backyard.

Piper took the long way home via the surface streets. She wanted to cruise, drive down main streets and try to focus on what her week would entail.

Her cell phone rang as she walked up the steps to her house. "Hello?" Piper said without looking at the caller ID.

"Hi, PJ. I was trying to catch you before you left. Would you be able to come into the office to discuss a few things about the house?" Renée asked.

Thrown off-guard, Piper replied, "Um, sure, Renée. I have few things to do in the morning but will swing by."

"Great, see you then," Renée said.

"See you then," Piper said and hung up.

If Renée wanted to speak to her about the house, that only meant she would no longer be the owner. Her father must have put the ball in motion for Savannah and Eric to purchase the home. Piper walked from the living space to the family room. She looked in every corner, doing a three-hundred-sixty-degree turn in each room. She walked through the kitchen to the back and through the laundry room. She entered the ground floor bedroom that doubled as her office. Nothing. No emotions. She realized she was not attached to this house at all.

Maybe this will be easier than I thought, Piper thought.

She could not think of one special moment she had shared with Scott in this house. No memories. She slogged upstairs to watch television and relax. She knew her upcoming week would be a big one.

ଔଓ

As the party at Daphne's home dispersed, Mr. and Mrs. Jackson realized they hadn't seen Piper in a while. They weren't overly protective, but Piper had a lot to deal with and they wanted to make sure she was having a normal day. Mr. and Mrs. Jackson said their farewells and left.

"Should we stop by and check on Piper?" Mrs. Jackson.

"No, let her rest. Today was an emotionally draining day for her," Mr. Jackson stated.

"That's why we should stop by: She may need us."

"The last thing she needs is us. She needs to be alone. She has a very big week ahead, and we are not sure how it will turn out."

"I just want to be there for my daughter, Brock."

"You will be. She's going to be staying with us while she has her treatments."

"And when was this agreed upon?" Mrs. Jackson asked.

"We spoke about the particulars the day I went for lunch."

"Well, let's go by the mall before going home. I want to have fresh new linen for her when she comes home."

They drove to the mall nearest Daphne. Not their usual shopping center, but for what they needed, it would do. It was small, with high-end stores. Macy's was on the north side, and Nordstrom's on the south, with boutique shops between them.

"Will Macy's do?" Mr. Jackson asked his wife.

"Yes, Macy's will do. I only want to grab a few things. I won't be long," Mrs. Jackson said.

Mr. Jackson parked directly in front of the store. It was nearly closing time and there were plenty of good parking spaces available. As he sat listening to jazz, thumbing the side of his driver's-side car door, he saw a familiar face. He was struggling with a baby, trying to get out of the door with a car seat atop a stroller and bags.

Mr. Jackson looked the young man in his face. Then he saw the woman with him. She was unfamiliar, but the man he knew. The man was Scott.

"My daughter is entering the most difficult time in her life and he's already begun a new one," he said to no one.

He watched as they crossed the narrow street to the parking lot.

Should I, or shouldn't I? Mr. Jackson asked himself. He stepped from the car. "Hello, Mr. Evans. How are you?" he said.

Scott's face dropped. Mr. Jackson could hear the cracking in his neck as he slowly lifted his head to look at Mr. Jackson.

Stuttering, Scott said, "M-M-Mr. Jackson?"

"In the flesh. And you, Ms. Are you a relative of Scott's?"

"Not yet," she said with a smile. "I'm Darla."

"I see. And this little bundle of joy in the stroller?" Mr. Jackson said as he snuck a peek under the blanket.

Scott took the blanket and raised it higher. "He's sleeping. I just took them to have their picture taken."

"Mr. Jackson, is it? Are you related to PJ?" she asked.

"Yes, Ms. I am. I'm her father. I'm also Scott's father-in-law."

"Really?" Darla said, surprised. "Scott, I thought PJ was just your high school girlfriend."

"We'll talk about this later, Darla," Scott said.

"I am so happy we met, Mr. Jackson." Darla took the baby and headed for her BMW, which was parked a few rows behind Mr. Jackson.

"Good seeing you, Mr. Jackson," Scott said as he tried to walk away.

"A word, Scott," Mr. Jackson said.

"Yes, sir?"

"For now, this conversation will be between you and I. Were you having an affair with this woman?"

Scott couldn't lie. He feared Mr. Jackson would hurt him. "Yes, sir."

"Is that your child?" Mr. Jackson asked.

"Please, sir. May I be the one to tell PJ? I don't want to hurt her any more than I already have."

"Yes, you have hurt my daughter, very deeply. In time, she will get over you. Piper is sick. She has a lot to worry about right now. She doesn't need or deserve this from you," Mr. Jackson stated.

"I made poor decisions that ultimately hurt everyone involved. Darla didn't know I was married to Piper. I thought it would just be a fling. She became pregnant, and I was forced to make a decision that I never thought I would ever have to make. That's my son, sir. And I am truly sorry for how I treated Piper. I didn't want to hurt her any more. I was planning on moving out of state, hoping she would forget about me, but things changed. Can I be the one to tell her? It's only right."

"I will give you that chance. But you will only get one chance," Mr. Jackson said.

"I need time. I will let you know when I plan to tell her," Scott said.

"Agreed. There's something else you need to consider," Mr. Jackson said.

"Yes, sir?"

"The house. You committed adultery. That will come out in a divorce hearing," Mr. Jackson said.

"I will have my father amend the divorce papers. I don't want anything to do with the house," Scott said.

"Agreed. Have a good evening, Scott. And do keep your word. That's usually the only thing a person like you have left," Mr. Jackson said.

"Yes, sir." Scott trotted off to the car.

Mr. Jackson could tell from his rearview mirror that Scott and Darla were having a lengthy conversation. Darla was sobbing profusely.

Mrs. Jackson returned to the car with several bags of linens and towels. "Now, I think I have everything. We should put Piper in the bedroom downstairs."

"Yeah, downstairs," Mr. Jackson said. He sped out of the parking space and drove away.

"Brock, why are you in a hurry? Let me put my seatbelt on," Mrs. Jackson complained.

Mr. and Mrs. Jackson lived in Palos Verdes Estates. The thirty-minute conversation Mr. Jackson held with his wife on the drive home was not memorable. He could only remember the words Scott had said: "He's my son." That just might kill Piper if she were to find out. Not only did he have an affair, but he had a child out of wedlock.

Mr. Jackson now had a secret. One he could not share with his wife — or anyone. Not yet, at least.

Chapter Eleven

The sound of jazz playing on her cell phone woke Piper. It was her father calling to make sure she was ready for her blood work.

"Dad, I can go alone. You can take me tomorrow, for chemo. I can have my blood drawn at the hospital where I work today. They will forward the results to the center. I have to go see Renée when I'm done."

"All right, Piper. I'll call you in the morning."

They hung up and Piper got ready for her day.

Piper had worked for Hampshire Hospital for three years. She would be able to complete her lab work there, if she liked. She opted not to have her chemo treatments there, as she knew most of the people and some of the frequent patients.

She had been to the lab many times in the past, but saw new faces when she approached the main desk to check in. The lab technician she was assigned to was athletically built and good-looking gentleman with the name "Monte" on his name tag.

Piper handed him her ticket with the particular information for the different types of lab work that he would be drawing. She wondered if he could tell she had cancer by the small tickets with bar codes on them.

"Name, please," Monte said while reaching for the different clear vials with different color tips.

He didn't look up until he heard "Piper Jackson-Evans."

His gaped when he looked up and saw Piper, dressed in a floral sundress, flop hat to match. "Mrs. Evans, please have a seat. Do you have a preference as to which arm I should use?"

"No, either one will do. But you only get one poke. If you don't get it the first time, you won't get a second chance."

"I can usually get it the first try," Monte said with a chuckle.

"Well, I have roving veins, so it may be a little difficult," she explained.

"Ah, thanks for telling me. Now I will make sure that I get it on the first try," Monte said, smiling.

Piper looked away as he slipped the needle into her vein without a pinch. He filled vial after vial.

"All done, Mrs. Evans."

"Please call me PJ. Everyone does. And it's Ms. Jackson."

"Ok, PJ. See you next time."

"Thanks, Monte."

Piper had not been interested in another man since she met Scott. She found herself somewhat attracted to Monte and thought if she saw him the next time, she would flirt, harmlessly.

She pulled the pink bandage off the crease of her elbow as she drove to Renée's office.

As she pulled into the parking lot, her cell phone received a text message. She pulled out her phone and shut the engine off. The message read: *Hey, PJ. I'm having my dad prepare amended divorce papers. I've decided that you should keep the house. I don't want any parts of it. You should receive the papers by courier later today. Will you be home?*

She read and reread the text message. *I wonder why he doesn't want any parts of the house, now. Daddy must have spoken to him. Great. One less thing to worry about.*

She replied: *No, leave it in the mailbox.*

Before she could get out the car, another text message came through. She rolled her eyes to the heavens and said sarcastically, "My goodness." She retrieved the message as she walked to Renée's office.

Scott: *How are you?*

Piper stopped in her tracks and repeated, "How am I?" Then replied: *What do you care?*

She turned off her cell phone and entered the building. Renée's family owned the real estate company. Everyone who worked there was either family or close friends.

"Hello," Piper said to the receptionist. "I'm here to see Renée."

"Hi, PJ, how are you?" the receptionist said.

Piper looked at the young woman and said, "I'm sorry, do we know each other?"

"Yes, I'm Renée's niece. Shelly. We met at the wedding! How are you?"

"Oh, yes, Shelly. My, you are a beautiful young lady now. You were a junior bridesmaid in the wedding."

"I'm well. I'm doing my internship here, for college credit."

Renée could hear Piper and Shelly talking from her office and stepped out to greet her. "PJ? Come on in. Good to see you," Renée said.

"Take care, Shelly, and it was really good seeing you," Piper said and stepped into Renée's office.

The office was elegant and sophisticated. There was a large map of the city on one wall and pictures of Renée and Davon on the others. Rena's picture occupied a space on her desk next to the computer.

"Now that Papa Jackson is helping Eric and Savannah purchase your home, it will make for a successful transaction," Renée said.

"Great," Piper replied.

"I still have the paperwork from when you purchased the home. With the improvements and upgrades you've done, you can get a really good price, as well as make it affordable to Eric and Savannah. Since they are currently renting, they want to be able to save a little extra money to help with the new addition to their family. With the funds they have and what Papa Jackson is giving them, they should be able to put a nice sum down and pay less for the mortgage than what they were paying in rent."

"Sounds great. Where do I sign?" Piper said.

"Don't you want to know the price and your profit?"

"I don't really care about that. Anything I get will be fine," Piper said.

"What about Scott's half? Should I contact him? You know he's going to have to sign the paperwork as well."

"If I have a signed statement saying I can keep the house, does he still have to sign? I can have his father take if before the judge to have it approved."

"Not if he has himself removed from the mortgage, he won't have to sign.," Renée said.

"Great. Now, hand me the paperwork and let me know when I need to begin packing."

Piper happily signed the papers Renée gave her. She looked at this as a new beginning. Not looking back on the past. Starting over. After she was free from cancer, she could begin a new life. One without Scott.

Piper went for a long walk when she got home. She had a big day ahead of her. First day of chemotherapy. As she walked, she listened to oldies on her headset. She wanted to concentrate on getting and being healthy for her treatments. A slow song by the Ojays played while she waited for the stoplight to change. Monte's face appeared as she closed her eyes. She was startled by the sound of loud music coming from a passing car. It snapped her out of her trance, back to reality.

She could not remember ever seeing Monte prior to today. *He must be a new technician*, Piper thought.

Trying to focus on her walk was no easy task. Visions of Monte enveloped her. She couldn't figure out why he was so heavy on her mind. They had just met. He drew her blood, that was it. So technically they didn't meet. Officially.

She trotted up the steps to her colonial-style home. *Well, it won't be too many more times that I'll be able to do this,* she thought.

She checked her mailbox. A manila envelope, too large to fit properly, was stuck in it. She took it out. The cover read: *Amended papers. Thanks PJ.*

Piper wanted to make sure she got the process over with as soon as possible. She read it briefly. *I wonder what Dad could have said to him to make him change his mind,* Piper thought as she signed the divorce agreement.

Tears fell from her eyes. She had thought their love was eternal. She didn't want the divorce but she felt forced into signing. And ultimately, she wanted to believe that this was best for her and Scott. For sure, Scott; for her, not so sure. After all, she was battling an illness that most people died from. An illness that she would have to battle alone. Of course, she had her family, but it didn't compare to the sensitive love of just someone rubbing the back of your neck because you said it didn't feel right. Or someone massaging your feet, because you were tired. Her family would do those things, but it wouldn't be the same kind of love.

She began her nightly routine before bed and decided to add a pity party on top of it. Her chemo appointment wasn't until one o'clock in the afternoon. That would give her plenty of time to sober up. As she made her way to the kitchen, her cell phone rang. She had a feeling that it was Scott and let the call go to voicemail.

When she returned to listen to the bull he had left on her phone, there was no message. The call came from a private number. *Maybe it was the hospital reminding me of my appointment. Oh, well, let the pity party begin!*

Chapter Twelve

"Who's ringing my phone at 6:00 a.m.?" Piper shouted as her cell rang an unfamiliar tune. It was someone she didn't know. "Private number?" she said as she looked at the caller ID.

"Good morning, this is Piper. How may I help you?" Piper said as if she were answering her work phone.

Heavy breathing was the only response. She looked at the phone and thought: *Who could this be? Maybe it's a wrong number.*

The caller hung up abruptly after the third hello.

"Weird," Piper said. She crawled out of bed.

She heard her doorbell ring, and keys jingling to open the front door. She didn't need to be The Amazing Kreskin to realize her father was there to take her to her first chemo appointment.

"Be down soon, Dad," Piper shouted.

"I'll wait in the kitchen. Do you have coffee ready?"

"Just hit the button on the coffee maker. It should be ready before I am," Piper yelled down.

After showering and getting dressed, she took a few selfies on her cell phone so that she could forever have this day, the day before her first chemo session, and remember how she looked.

"Piper, you ready yet? You know this is a heavy traffic day," Mr. Jackson said.

"Coming, Dad!" Piper trotted downstairs to join her father.

"Are you packed?" Mr. Jackson asked.

"What do you mean, packed?" Piper asked quizzically.

"We spoke about this! You're coming home with me to stay the night, so that your mom and I can keep an eye on what side-effects you may have, if any."

"Let me grab a few things. Be right back." Piper jogged up the steps and grabbed a few sweat suits, undergarments, pajamas, and toiletries.

"Let's go, Dad," she said as she came down the steps with an overnight bag.

"Do you have the directions programmed in your GPS in the Lexus?" asked Mr. Jackson.

"Yeah, why?"

"Come on, you drive your car and I'll drive the return trip. It's early and I need a nap," Mr. Jackson said.

With a chuckle, Piper said, "Sure, Dad. And thank you for taking me to my appointment."

"Wouldn't have it any other way," Mr. Jackson said.

Piper listened to a book she had downloaded instead of music, to spare her father the traumatic experience of listening to rap on their long drive to the Cheryl Lincoln Research and Oncology Center.

Before exiting the freeway, Piper tapped her father on the shoulders to let him know they were about to arrive.

Mr. Jackson took a wet nap and refreshed his face after his two-hour nap. "Are you sure you're in the right place, Piper? This looks like a resort with a large park in the back."

Piper pulled up to the valet. Two men approached each side of the car and opened the doors to help Piper and her dad out of the car. "May I have your name, please?" one of the gentlemen said.

"Piper Jackson."

He wrote her name on the ticket and directed them to the automatic doors that led inside the building.

Mr. Jackson looked around the inside of the center, turning right and left, and said, "This is really nice, Piper."

Piper checked in at the front desk and was told to have a seat until her name was paged.

They sat in the area where the large flat-screen TV played old movies on the TCM channel. "My kind of movies!" Mr. Jackson said.

Piper had never been so nervous before in her life. The only sound she could hear was her own heartbeat. He father reached out and grabbed her and said, "We are all cut from the same cloth. We are strong. You can do this. I'm here with you and will not leave you."

She turned to her father and said, "Thank you, Daddy. I needed that." She kissed him on the cheek.

From the corner of her eye, she saw someone coming toward her. It was Doctor Cheung.

She stood and greeted her doctor and introduced him to her father. They shook hands and the doctor led them to the elevator. When they arrived, Dr. Cheung took them to the infusion suite. The doctor directed Piper to one of the private rooms.

"For your first time, Piper, I suggest you and your dad use this room. If you need anything while receiving your infusion, just press this button and your nurse should arrive directly. She will be here shortly to take your vitals. I received your test results from the blood work and everything looks good. Once we take your vitals, the nurse will begin an I.V. You will be given medicine to reduce the nausea first. Once that's completed, they will start the cocktail for your treatment. Do you have any questions?"

"Do you know how long it will take?"

"A few hours. Let's see how you react to the medicine and then it will become a regular routine. Here's the remote for the TV. And again, someone will be here soon," Dr. Cheung said.

"Thank you," Piper and Mr. Jackson said in unison.

Mr. Jackson channel surfed, looking for the channel that had been playing on the downstairs television. When the nurse entered the room with I.V. bags and needles, reality set in. He moved his chair closer to Piper so that she could grab his hand, if need be. He knew how much Piper hated needles.

"Hello, Ms. Jackson. I'm Rachel and I'll be your nurse for the day."

"Hello, Rachel, this is my dad, Mr. Jackson, and he'll be staying with me today."

She held out her hand to shake his.

"It's a pleasure, Ms. Rachel."

"Ready to get started?" Rachel asked Piper.

"As ready as I'm going to be," Piper said.

Rachel looked for a vein in Piper's arm to begin the I.V. "Did Dr. Cheung give you the particulars?" she asked Piper.

"Yes, he did," Piper said.

"That's good. I'll start by administering the medication to prevent nausea. Then the chemo cocktail."

"Thank you" was all Piper managed to say.

"You okay, Piper?" her dad asked.

"Yes. I'm all right."

Shortly after the nausea medication, Rachel began the chemotherapy cocktail. "Please let me know if you feel nauseated or sick."

"Sure," Piper said.

Expecting an instant change, Piper sat on pins and needles, watching the drops. With every drop, the cancer would decrease. She felt a jolt of excitement, believing that this would work. She would only have to endure this for a while and then she could begin life all over again.

She was so focused on watching the medicine flow from her I.V. that she hadn't noticed her dad step out of the room. Shortly after, the nurse returned to remove her I.V.

"How do you feel?" Rachel asked.

"It's weird, but I feel refreshed," Piper said. "Have you seen my dad?"

"He was pacing in the hall. I believe he was just a little nervous for you. I'll let him know you're done. Go to the checkout counter to schedule your next appointment."

"Great, I'm looking forward to it," Piper said excited.

She left the private room and found her father pacing the hallway, talking on his cell phone. "Yes, the facility is nice and clean. She should be done soon. Yes, I know it took a while, but the first one is in the books," Piper overheard her father say.

"You ready?" she said as she walked up behind him.

"She's done. Be home soon, hon," Mr. Jackson said as he hung up.

"Was that Mom?" Piper asked.

"Yes. You know your mother is a worrywart."

"Mom's a worrywart?" Piper said sarcastically. "Nooo!" They both smiled.

"I'm feeling really good, Dad. I think I can drive home," Piper said.

"Are you sure? That was an awful long treatment," he replied.

"Yeah, but I feel fine."

"Well, that's good news."

They headed to the valet. Mr. Jackson tipped him twenty dollars when he arrived with the car.

Piper had had her cell phone off during her treatment so that she wouldn't be distracted. She discovered she had a voicemail from a private number. Anxiously, she retrieved it. She had no idea who could be trying to reach her from a private number. She decided to listen to the message as her cell phone connected to her car's Bluetooth.

"Hello, um, PJ? I mean, Piper. You don't know me, but I need to speak to you. It is very urgent. It's not appropriate to tell you in a voice message. I will just try and call back at a later time. Um, thank you."

To Piper, the voice was hurried and unfamiliar. Mr. Jackson listened with a curious ear.

"Who could that be?" Piper said aloud.

Mr. Jackson knew. He knew exactly who it was. She had been with his ex–son-in-law the last time he saw her.

Chapter Thirteen

The drive home was quiet. Piper thought endlessly about the phone call. *Who is this person? And what would she want with me?*

Mr. Jackson felt an uneasy pain in his stomach. He looked sick.

"Dad, are you all right?" Piper asked.

"I'm fine. Just a little motion sickness. That's all," Mr. Jackson replied.

"We're near the house. Do you want to stop and get something for your stomach?"

"No. Your mom is well-stocked. She knows you're coming today and is prepared for any- and everything. She went through this with Daphne. She knows exactly what you'll need."

Piper just shook her head. She imagined her former bedroom set up as a hospital room, complete with rolling tray table that swung across the bed. A bedside table full of pharmaceuticals and a basin nearby.

They pulled in front of the two-story craftsman home Mr. and Mrs. Jackson had occupied for many years. Mr. Jackson retrieved Piper's overnight bag from the trunk of her car, and they entered the house through the side door that led them through the family room.

Since the Jackson children had their own dwellings, Mrs. Jackson had designed her living room as if it were a museum exhibit of her children, with pictures and framed accomplishments. The living room was hardly ever occupied. It had to be a very special occasion for anyone to occupy it.

Mrs. Jackson was seated in the den, where the family gathered on a regular basis. Dinner was cooking on the stove and the house was immaculate.

"Smells good, Mom," Piper said.

Mrs. Jackson rose to the sound of Piper's voice. "How are you feeling, Piper?"

"I'm good, Mom. Really, I am," she said.

"Are you hungry? Dinner's about ready. Meatloaf, mashed potatoes with gravy, green beans and cornbread."

"Sounds good, Mom. Give me a minute to get refreshed." Piper took her bags and went upstairs to her old bedroom.

"How did it go, Brock?" Mrs. Jackson asked.

"She said she feels good," he answered.

"Are you ready to eat? I'll prepare your plate," said Mrs. Jackson.

"Thanks, dear. Let me get cleaned up. I'll be back."

Mr. Jackson went to his bedroom to make a phone call, one that he dreaded. "Scott, its Papa Jackson," he said to Scott's answering service. "Please return my call. It's urgent. Thank you."

Mr. Jackson washed his hands and returned to the kitchen. As he sat at the table, his cell phone rang. It was Scott, returning his call. He decided to send the call to his voicemail. He didn't want to have to explain to his wife nor lie to her about speaking with Scott.

Mrs. Jackson gave Mr. Jackson his plate and they began eating dinner.

"I'm going to ask the boys to meet me at Piper's this evening so that we can begin packing her up," Mr. Jackson said.

"Good. The sooner the better," Mrs. Jackson said.

Piper entered as Mr. Jackson finished his dinner. "How's dinner? Good as usual?" Piper asked her father.

"Your mom outdid herself with this one. I believe she wanted to show you she still had it after all these years."

"Thanks, Mom, for everything." Piper said and gave her mom a hug.

"Here, have a seat and I'll fix you a nice healthy plate."

"Great," Piper said.

"Piper, I'm calling your brothers over tonight. We're going to start moving your things over here. Did you prepare the list I asked for? Things that are being moved from your house to ours and what's going in storage," Mr. Jackson asked.

"No list needed. I'm leaving everything. Savannah and Eric are buying a furnished home. I don't want anything other than my personal belongings. My clothes, computer, books, and toiletries. That's it." Piper ate. Her mother watched. She waited, anticipated her getting sick. Piper felt her mother watching and decided not to continue eating. "Mom, I'm fine. I don't feel nauseated."

Mrs. Jackson retreated to the kitchen, defeated. She washed dishes. Piper heard her sniffle. She had hoped her mother wasn't crying. She didn't want the pampering, and she didn't want to hurt her mother's feelings either. She decided that she would wash the dishes, just to prove to her mother she was fine. "Mom, I'll do the dishes."

"Are you sure, sweetheart?"

"Mom, really, I'm fine," Piper said.

Piper finished the dishes, washed down the refrigerator and stove. She cleaned the dining table of any crumbs that might have been left behind.

She decided to rest for a while. She trotted up the stairs. She made it halfway up, got instantly nauseated. She swayed a little, feeling as if she would faint. She called to her parents. "Mom! Dad!"

Her father ran to the stairway. Mrs. Jackson was taking garbage out to the bins in the backyard and had not heard Piper's cry.

"Madeline!" Mr. Jackson yelled to his wife as he ran up the steps.

Piper fell to the ground as he reached out to her. She didn't pass out. She was just weak. The side effects of chemo. She vomited profusely.

"MADELINE!" he yelled again. He sat on the floor with Piper's head in his lap.

Mrs. Jackson yelled. "What is it, Brock?" as she came through the back door.

"It's Piper," Mr. Jackson said.

Mrs. Jackson ran toward the stairs. "Oh, my lord," she cried. "Is she breathing, Brock?"

"She's just sick, Madeline. Get her a cold towel."

Piper laid her head across her father's lap. She couldn't move. Even though she had just eaten, her stomach was now empty. "I need some water," she managed to say to her father.

"Get Piper a bottle of water," he called out to his wife.

Mrs. Jackson returned with an armful of wet and dry towels, a bottle of water, and cleaning solution for the carpet.

"Carry her to her room, Brock," Mrs. Jackson said. "I'll move everything later."

Mr. Jackson lifted Piper in one swoop and took her to the bedroom.

"I'll be there when I'm done cleaning the steps. I'll give her a bath and get her ready for bed," Mrs. Jackson said.

Mr. Jackson laid Piper on top of the bed. At that moment, Piper felt satisfied that she had finally had a reaction to today's dilemma. She wondered if all her chemo days would be this way. The beige walls were welcome over the vibrant shades of lavender that had colored them when she had last occupied the room. She felt safe. She was home.

Her mother applied a cold compress to her head. Her dad excused himself. The ordeal he had just witnessed had him more determined than ever to speak with Scott. He didn't want anyone, especially Scott's friend, to add stress to his daughter's life. Not now, not while she was in a battle for her life. That he would not tolerate.

He went to the garage where he could speak to Scott in peace. The missed phone call had resulted in a voice message. He listened to the message first before trying to return Scott's call.

The voice was a female's. The message plainly stated: "If you're looking for Scott Evans, he's currently unavailable. Please accept his apologies." And the message ended. Same voice, different demeanor. There was an apparent attitude in her tone.

Mr. Jackson dialed Scott's cell phone again. This time, it was answered. "Mr. Evans' phone. May I help you?" she said.

"Yes, this is Mr. Brock Jackson. Is Mr. Evans available? It is imperative that I speak with him."

"I'm sorry, Mr. Jackson, Scott is out of town and he left his cell phone behind. Can I take a message? This is his wife, Darla."

Mr. Jackson was stunned. It had only been a few weeks since Scott was married to his daughter. The divorce was not yet final. *Maybe she just referred to herself as his wife.*

"No. No message. But can you tell me, Mrs. Evans, when he will return?"

"He's on a business trip, and I'm not sure when he'll be returning."

"Thank you for your time," Mr. Jackson said.

The woman hung up.

It was time to put his daughter's life back together. He wanted to start with her home. He called his sons and they decided to meet at Piper's house around six the following evening. Mr. Jackson had zero tolerance for tardiness. High school teacher training. His sons would be prompt. He also called Eric and Sherwin to see if they were available to help.

When he met his sons at Piper's house, they planned strategically how they could simplify the move. They started with her bedroom and took her belongings from the closet.

"I want everything completed tonight," Mr. Jackson stated.

Davon arrived with his wife and daughter to help pack. Piper was in no mood to do it and she was more than happy to allow her sister-in-law and niece to help out. They would be responsible for her personal items. Her niece, Rena, spent more time trying on Piper's high heel shoes than packing them.

The truck they rented made the hauling easy. They packed her clothing in wardrobe boxes that could be stored in the garage temporarily until Piper felt like unpacking. The trips in and out of the house were not many, but Mr. Jackson felt his age. He decided to let the younger generation complete the packing while he supervised. Rena was in charge of keeping the men hydrated.

Mr. Jackson sat on the front porch, welcoming the cool night air. When there was a change in activity, people noticed. Piper's neighbors were looking curiously at what was happening at her home. While it was not unusual for people to watch when someone was moving, it was unusual for them to sit in a car and watch every move that was being made.

Drinking his water, Mr. Jackson noticed the dark blue BMW down the street. A woman sat behind the wheel and watched the comings and goings at Piper's house. She sat and stared. She wanted Mr. Jackson to see her. She made sure of it. She stared as if she had a beam of light penetrating his skin until he noticed her. Once they made eye contact, she drove off, watching him intently. He knew now, at that moment, that her intentions were not good. She wanted to hurt Piper and he would not allow that.

Chapter Fourteen

The house was packed and Piper was ready to settle into her old room. She didn't want to stay in the bedroom her mother offered her, downstairs.

The garage, which had plenty of space, was packed with wardrobe boxes. Piper didn't like the idea of having to get her clothing from the garage to dress, so she made a date with her sister Harmony to help her unpack her belongings so that she could get settled before her next chemo appointment.

She was thrilled not to have to return to her home. She had put the thought of it out of her mind. She was beginning to feel that her marriage was just a farce. She hoped never to dwell on her house or her marriage ever again.

Her home was now ready for Savannah and Eric to rent. Mr. Jackson would pay the mortgage and Eric and Savannah would pay him. The pricey furniture Piper left behind was very much wanted. Savannah and Eric kept their bedroom furniture and donated Piper's to a homeless shelter.

"Keep what you want," Piper had said to them. "If you don't like it, you can get rid of it."

The weekend before Piper's next appointment was the day she and Harmony decided they would get her settled into her old room at their parents' home.

They unpacked box after box. Many of Piper's outfits reminded her one way or another of Scott: where they had gone when she wore her green lace dress, or what event they had attended when she wore her black strapless cocktail dress.

"I think I need to do a little house cleaning," Piper said. "The outfits in this pile I will donate to the women's shelter in Long Beach for battered and abused women. I think I want to change up my style."

She came across a beautiful cream-colored dress with angel sleeves that Scott's father had given her when Scott's mother passed away. Piper always admired her fashion sense.

"Are you going to give that one away?" Harmony asked with excitement in her voice. The dress was simply beautiful, and Harmony wanted it for herself if Piper was going to get rid of it.

"No," Piper said in a low tone. "I love that dress. Scott's mother wanted to be buried in it when she found out she was dying. She told me so. She had hoped her husband would remember that one request. But Scott's dad decided against the dress and purchased a new one for her. She left him instructions that she wanted me to have most of her expensive clothes and suits since we wore the same size. I was in awe when his dad gave it to me after she was buried. This reminds me so much of her and how special our relationship was. I think she was the best thing I can say I had in my marriage."

Piper looked at the dress from the front to the back, admiring all the little details. "This one is a keeper," she said.

They continued to sort her clothes, placing some in the shelter pile and others in a keeper pile, in complete silence. Harmony broke it to ask Piper about her first chemo visit.

"All in all, the actual appointment went well. It wasn't until hours later that I felt sick. I think Mom was just a tad bit happy that I needed her to attend to me, so for that I'm grateful."

"Oh, PJ. I'm sorry. I'm here for you if you need me."

"I'm fine, Harm. Just a little sickness. It's to be expected. Let's not discuss my life. Let's talk wedding plans."

"Well, you know our second mom wants to go with me to look for a dress. Daphne always have to feel as if she's a big part of whatever is going on in our lives. I wonder what she would be like if she didn't have daughters of her own to fuss over."

"In Daphne's mind, she has four daughters: Savannah, Sabrina, you, and me," Piper said jokingly.

"I know, and she's just like Mom. When we're done, let's get online and take a look at a few bridesmaid dresses."

"Sure," Piper said.

They completed the unpacking and loaded the boxes for the shelter. "I believe I may need to do a little shopping for myself," Piper said.

"We can take care of that later," Harmony said. "I really want to spend a little alone time, here with you. Looking at bridesmaid dresses."

"Let's get the laptop and do a little research. Do you have dresses in mind? Do you know how many women and who will be in your party?"

"Well, let me see. You, Sabrina and my future sisters-in-law."

Piper reminisced about her nuptials. Savannah and Sabrina had been junior bridesmaids and Harmony the maid of honor. Oh, how happy she had been that day. To finally marry the man of her dreams. "What a waste," Piper said out loud.

"You think four bridesmaids are too many?" Harmony asked.

"No. Just thinking out loud," Piper replied.

Harmony looked at her sister, and for the first time since Piper had announced that she and Scott were no longer together, she saw her true heart break.

"Let's do this another time," Harmony suggested.

"Whatever," Piper said, obviously irritated at the thought of marriage.

Harmony gathered her belongings, bid her parents a farewell, and left.

Piper welcomed the solitude. No matter how hard she tried, no matter how mad she got, the thought of Scott angered her. She never saw divorce. She saw a beautiful home with a white picket fence and his and hers children. Her once fairytale life had turned into a nightmare.

She recalled her life from the day they were married, to try to figure out just when her husband had fallen out of love with her. She searched her mind and heart. Her cell phone interrupted her thoughts.

"Thinking of the devil," she said aloud. "What is it, Scott?"

"Hey PJ, please don't hang up."

She looked at the phone. It was Scott's number, but the voice was not Scott's.

"Who is this?" she said with more curiosity than worry in her voice.

"My name is Darla, and I'm, um, a friend of Scott's."

Piper's heart raced. She didn't know what to think. In her few seconds of silence, her heart skipped three beats. She managed to say in a low tone, "Is Scott all right?"

"He's fine. My call is not about Scott."

"Then why are you calling me? I'm no longer his wife."

"Yes, I know. Scott and I are engaged. And I wanted to be the one to tell you. Scott doesn't like to do emotional things like this, so I told him I would make the call for him."

Now, with anger in her voice, Piper responded, "And you're telling me because?"

Silence.

"Are you there?" Piper asked.

"Yes, I'm here. Look, I don't want to cause any problems. I just thought you should know." And Darla hung up.

She didn't know why a woman named Darla was calling her and why she was engaged to her former husband of just a few weeks. She knew of no one named Darla.

There were two scenarios: One, she was a woman Scott had been seeing for some time during their marriage; or two, she was playing high school games just to get under Piper's skin.

Piper needed sleep. She had to have her blood drawn and go for chemotherapy the following day. She went to sleep with the thought that Darla was playing games with her. She didn't know why. Maybe Scott put her up to it. She couldn't dwell on this now. She had her health and her life to consider, and she needed to put Scott out of her mind and out of her heart for good.

Chapter Fifteen

The lie she told her parents, to enable her to go to her appointment alone, was only a little white lie, Piper told herself. With the drive being a long one, she needed the meditation. She didn't need any distractions. Her heart wanted to call Scott and ask who Darla was, but her head knew better.

"Scott and I are engaged," echoed in Piper's head during the short drive to the hospital. It wasn't until she parked her car at the hospital to have her blood drawn that she was reminded of Monte, the handsome, charismatic phlebotomist who had drawn her blood her last visit.

At the reception desk, she contemplated asking for him directly. Instead she remained hopeful that she would have the luck of the draw.

"Please have a seat in the waiting area and wait for your number to be called. It may take longer than usual," said the blond receptionist.

"Thank you," Piper said in return.

She turned and saw a fairly attractive young woman of about twenty-two or -three years of age, with what Piper called "the look of death" in her eyes. Sunken, hollow, and dark. From her nursing experience as an ER nurse, Piper knew it would not be long before she would die. The yellow bandana tied around her head indicated that she had lost hair from cancer treatments. Piper said a humble prayer in silence for the nameless young woman and took a seat next to her.

"And how are you this morning?" Piper asked while taking a seat.

"I'm hanging in there. How about yourself? How are you?" she asked.

"Good," Piper said. "Will be better once my treatments are complete, but you gotta do what you gotta do!" Piper said.

"Well, good luck with that," the young lady said with a weak smile.

Piper stared at her. Her head was bowed nearly to her knees. She was obviously frail and miserable.

"If you don't mind me asking, how old are you?" Piper asked.

"Eighteen last month," she said. "And you?"

"I'm twenty-five," Piper said. "Are you in school? College?"

"I was, until my relapse. I have leukemia. My brother is here with me to get tested, to see if he's a match. I need a bone marrow transplant. Or my outcome will not be that great."

"I'm sorry — Um, I didn't get your name?"

"It's Shelia."

"I'm Piper, but you can call me PJ."

"Nice to meet you, PJ. I'm hopeful I will survive this. I've suffered from this disease off and on for years. I still have some fight in me."

"Well, you fight. And you fight hard. Don't give in and don't give up. You are young and beautiful and have a lot of life to live."

"Thank you. I will," Shelia said.

"Number twenty to Area A" was heard over the loudspeaker. The young women glanced at her ticket and said, "That's me."

The gentleman that sat on the other side of her must have been her brother. He walked to the back of the room and retrieved a wheelchair. He helped her up and into it.

"You take care of yourself," Piper said.

The young woman gave her a thumbs-up with a weak smile as she made her way behind the double doors.

Piper could not get over the fact that this woman was only eighteen and near the end of her life.

Piper waited endlessly for her turn. She had hoped she would have the Monte person as her technician. She didn't understand the attraction she had for him. All she knew was that since the day he drew her blood, he had been on her mind more than he should be.

Piper stood when she heard her number called. She rushed to the area in the hopes of seeing Monte. Instead she saw an older woman of about fifty with granny glasses hanging on the tip of her nose.

"Piper Jackson?" she asked Piper as she walked in.

"Yes, I'm Piper."

"Have a seat. Which arm do you prefer?"

"No preference," Piper said. She glanced around the laboratory. She saw women and men in white lab coats, some testing blood, others drawing it. She saw one young man that she thought might be Monte, but as he approached, she realized he was not as handsome.

"All done. Keep this bandage on for at least twenty minutes."

"Thank you," Piper said and headed out.

Her chemo appointment wasn't until three o'clock. She had a few hours to kill before taking the long drive to the center.

She sat on a nearby bench to rest before driving. She pulled out her cell phone and thumbed through her apps until she reached her Book of Prayers. She searched for a prayer to say for Shelia. She didn't know her story. She only knew she felt an overwhelming heartache for her. So young and having to fight cancer.

She finished her prayer and added a couple of intentions for her own heath and her sanity. She felt a dark shadow fall over her from behind. The sun was hidden by the tall figure. As she turned slowly, she heard a voice say, "Hello, PJ." Monte had noticed her sitting alone on the bench.

"Hello, Monte," Piper said as she held her hand up to shield her eyes from the sun.

"Do you mind if I sit down?"

Piper slid over to the end of the bench. "Sure, have a seat," she said.

"How have you been since we last saw one another?" Monte asked.

"Good. Life's great. Always looking forward to the next day," Piper replied.

"Why wouldn't you look forward to the next day?" Monte asked.

"Well, when you're sick, you just never know."

"I'm not your doctor, but I do work at the hospital, so technically, I can't talk about your illness."

"It's okay. I don't mind. We can talk about it. It's only temporary," Piper said.

Monte looked her in her eyes to see if he could find something in them that would tell her story.

"Why don't we talk about me," Monte said in hopes of making Piper more comfortable.

"Okay, I have a little time to kill."

"Well, you know where I work. I'm twenty-seven years of age. Divorced and a single parent of a precious six-year-old named Harley."

"And you're telling me this because?"

"Just holding a conversation. Do you mind if I ask you a personal question?"

"Shoot!" Piper said.

"Are you married?"

"Not anymore," Piper said and she rolled her eyes to the sky.

"How long?"

"What time is it?" she asked, laughing.

Monte gave her a dubious look.

"I'm sorry. I'm recently divorce. My husband found out I had cancer and he left me. He blamed me and my cancer for us not being able to conceive a child during our marriage," Piper said.

"I'm sorry, PJ," Monte said with his heart truly filled with sorrow.

"Not your fault," she assured him.

"I know, but it does explain some things."

"Yeah, like what?" she asked.

"The sadness in your eyes. The sarcasm in your voice. You are a beautiful woman, PJ, on the outside. And I just bet it gets better once someone knows your heart. You're hiding behind the hurt. May I make a suggestion?" He continued without waiting for her answer. "Let him go. He didn't deserve you. Any man that walks out on his wife because she's ill is not a man. He's doing it to cover up something else. It's an excuse."

Piper looked at him as if he was telling her, her life story. He reached up and wiped the tears that she didn't realize had fallen down her cheeks.

At that moment, they both felt the electricity they shared when he touched her. She looked deeply into his eyes to search for his soul. It was there. She saw it. He was hurt and needed comfort just as she did.

"My turn to ask you a personal question?" Piper said.

"She cheated. She had an affair and realized that she wanted to live a life with no holds. She didn't want our daughter. She wanted freedom," he said as if he read her mind.

"I was only going to ask you what kind of car you drive."

He looked at her, eyebrows furrowed.

"I'm only kidding," she said. "How do you know me so well and this is just the second time we've set eyes on each other?"

"You think this is the second time? I've seen you walk the halls for years. I know you're a nurse here. I've been watching you, from a distance. You carry yourself very well, and I was attracted to you from the first day I saw you two years ago."

"Wow, I need to get eyes in the back of my head," Piper said.

"You didn't see me because you weren't looking. You were married. Now that you're divorced, your eyes are open and you can see what you didn't see when you were married."

To Piper's ears, his words were like a harp that played a beautiful melody. She wanted to know Monte. He was like her private psychiatrist. He was the cure for her broken heart.

"I have to go. I have an appointment and it's pretty far away," Piper said.

"Do you mind if we stay in touch? I wouldn't want to only talk to you when you come to have blood drawn," Monte said.

"Give me your cell number and I'll text you so that you will have mine," Piper replied.

"Cool," Monte said with the most beautiful smile across his handsome face. "I'm off at six. Mind if I call tonight?"

Piper thought about her chemo session last week and decided that calling the following day was better. He smiled, waved good-bye, and headed for the hospital.

Piper had a lot to think about during her hour-long drive. Monte, Monte, Monte…

Chapter Sixteen

Chemo sucks. Piper felt the effects the following day. She was tired, didn't have the energy to get out of bed. The ride home was an easy one — she felt fine. She managed to eat her dinner salad, but the aftereffects of *this* treatment were horrendous. She vomited until there was nothing left to come up. The sweating and shaking were unbearable. She was in and out of the bathroom. She showered and washed her hair. Her body felt as if it had not seen water in days. It was then that she noticed her hair was falling out. She was too tired and didn't want to deal with it. She had known that losing her hair was a possibility. She was just beginning to do so. Instead of wearing a wig, she had planned to wear a head scarf, one that would complement the outfit she wore for the day.

Allowing her mother to spoil and pamper her today was not a problem. She was actually looking forward to it. She was not up to seeing visitors, and her mother played the warden with her siblings. Brock Jr., Daphne, Davon, and Harmony were not allowed to visit this day.

"Piper needs her rest. She needs to regain her strength," her mother had told them.

Piper couldn't think straight. She thought she had made a date with Monte but was confused about the place. It took hours before she realized it was a phone date that they had scheduled.

When her cell phone rang, she sent it straight to voicemail. She didn't have the strength to talk to him, nor did she want to explain to him what her day was like.

By nightfall, she had managed to get out of bed and go downstairs.

Her parents were in their nightly spot, the dimly lit den, watching television.

"Hey," she said to them.

Her mother turned in her lounge chair. "Why are you out of bed? Are feeling any better?"

"I'm much better. Just a little sluggish," she replied.

Mr. Jackson did not turn around to look at her. He had a way of wearing his heart on his sleeve. He knew of the hair loss because his wife had mentioned it. He could not show Piper how he felt. "Do you need anything?" he asked without turning around.

"No, Daddy. I'm fine," she said. "I just needed to get out that room."

She walked into the kitchen and opened the refrigerator — just to look, not looking for anything in particular. Not wanting to be in her room. Realizing it was just as boring downstairs as it was up, she decided to retreat to her room.

She thought of Monte. Their last conversation was vague in her memory, but she did remember. She figured there was a lot she needed to think about before seeing him or wanting to see him again. *Am I truly attracted to him? Is it too soon to date after the disaster marriage I just had?*

"Piper?" her mother called out as she opened the bedroom door.

"Yes, Mom," she replied.

"This letter came by messenger today." She handed Piper an envelope that read "The Law Firm of Evans and Evans."

"Thanks," Piper said, staring at the envelope. She opened it slowly as her mother watched with folded arms.

"My divorce is final," Piper said.

"That was quick."

"It didn't take long because we were married in Las Vegas and his dad took care of everything."

"I see. Do you want to be alone? I can stay if you like," her mother offered.

"No, Mom. I'm fine. Thanks for offering. I need to make a few phone calls. Do you mind?" Piper said with eyes full of tears.

"Sure, baby," she said as she left the room.

Overcome with unexpected emotions, Piper cried and cried. And cried some more. "It's really over. Why Scott, why?" she shouted.

A vision of a woman came to her behind closed lids. A beautiful young woman, mouthing the words, "I'm his fiancée."

She opened her eyes, immediately expecting to see her, but all she saw through clouded eyes were cream-colored walls. She was back to reality. *She is single and sick. What would it hurt if she were to talk to Monte?* she thought. She picked up her cell phone and looked through her missed calls until she found Monte's number. *It's still early enough to call*, Piper thought. She hit redial.

"Hello?" the voice on the other end of the line said.

Piper, still emotional, could barely utter, "Monte?"

"Yes, PJ. Is everything all right? I can barely hear you," he said.

"No, I'm not all right. I could really use a friend right now."

"Do you want me to stop by? I can get my mom to watch Harley."

"I'm staying with my parents. I'm not sure how they will react."

"What's wrong? Can you tell me over the phone?"

"I guess I have good news. My divorce is final."

An awkward silence filled the line.

"Hello, are you there, Monte?"

"Yes, I'm here. I'm just not sure how to respond. How do you feel about that?" he asked.

"It wasn't a shock. I was just notified at a bad time. I knew it would be quick. I guess, just not that quick."

"Do you want to talk about it? I'll listen to anything you want to tell me."

Piper started crying again.

"How about this: I'll come and pick you up and we'll go for a drive out to the beach. That's my favorite place to go and meditate about life."

"I would like that. It's my favorite place as well. Give me an hour to get ready. I'll text you my address. Monte?"

"Yes?"

"You sure you don't mind?"

"What are friends for!" he replied.

That comforted Piper in an awkward way. A man she was curious about was willing to talk to her about her ex-husband. This would be interesting, if nothing else.

She texted Monte her parents' address. She also forwarded Harmony Monte's cell number and work location. *Mama didn't raise no fools. Better safe than sorry,* Piper thought and hit Send.

She waited three minutes for Harmony to reply: *Got it! And who's Monte?*

Piper responded with: *I'll tell you later.*

Harmony: *I take it you're feeling better?*

Piper: *Somewhat.*

Harmony: *Be safe!*

Piper: *Always*!

Piper put on a jogging suit and rushed downstairs to inform her parents that she was stepping out for a while.

"Where are you going?" her mother asked.

"That's none of your business!" her father chided.

"With a friend, Mom. I just need a little fresh air," Piper said.

"Is it someone...?" her mother began.

"Have a good time," her father interjected, looking sternly at her mother.

Piper was suddenly reminded why she had married so early: It was to get out of her parents' home.

"I will, Dad. Mom, don't worry. I'll be fine."

Piper's phoned buzzed in her pocket. She read the text. *I'm here. Are you sure I can't come in and meet your parents?*

Her only response was *OMW*.

She left the house, not looking back at her mother, whose eyes never left Piper. She envisioned her mother looking out the window watching for her to get into the car. As Monte opened the passenger-side door, Piper turned and saw the kitchen curtain sway.

"Hello, PJ," Monte said.

"There's a café around the corner. Can we go there instead of the beach?" Piper asked.

"Of course," he said. "Was that your mom looking out the window?"

"Yeah. She's a nervous Nellie!"

"Is that why she was looking like she was trying to get the license plate number of my car?"

"I'm sure she got the make, model, and color of your car, and probably a description of you, too. Sometimes I think she's overprotective, but more likely, she's just being nosey. I didn't tell her who I was going out with, which is probably eating at her right about now."

Monte stopped at a red light and turned to admire Piper. "How are you feeling?" he said.

"A little better now that I'm not alone."

"Is this the place?" Monte asked as he pulled his car to the curb in front of Mom's Donuts and Coffee Shop.

"Yes, let's go in," Piper said.

Chapter Seventeen

Mom's was a retro donut shop that served vintage coffee, as well as lattés and cappuccinos. A jukebox near the front door played music from the seventies. Patrons sat at the counter sipping coffee and eating donuts. Others sat in booths that lined the wall. Laptops were open on several tabletops. Some were enjoying the company of others. The smell of pastries and donuts was enough to make your blood sugar rise fifty points.

Piper suggested they take a vacant booth in the back.

Monte extended his hand to allow Piper to sit first. He took the bench opposite her. A young man of about eighteen approached them and welcomed them to the coffee shop. "Hi, I'm Daniel. Can I assist you with your order today?" he asked.

"I'll have the green tea, no sugar," Piper said.

"Black coffee for me," Monte said.

"Sure. It will be up in a second," Daniel informed them.

"Piper, let me start by saying, I think you are one classy woman. I have watched you from afar and have admired you for a long time. I know we have not known each other long, but I feel a special connection to you. The first time you came to my station, I could not believe it was you. I believe we were destined to meet, to be in this moment at this time. No matter what, I want us to be friends always," Monte confessed.

Piper's eyes filled with tears. She could not remember the last time she had been treated so kindly by a man she wasn't related to.

"What would you like to talk about?" he asked.

"I don't understand what could have happened between Scott and me," Piper managed to say. "We grew up together and married after high school. The first two years were like a honeymoon. Then Scott wanted children and I never conceived. I guess he was right. Maybe my illness did have something to do with it."

"No, Piper. I don't believe that at all. If it was meant to be, then it would have happened."

Daniel returned to the table with their drinks.

"God doesn't make mistakes. If you were going to be a mother, it would have been so."

"Is that what you believe? Do you think God gave you a child so that you can raise her alone?" Piper asked.

"This is His plan for me, to be her father. I don't have any regrets, especially when it comes to her mother. I guess you can say she and I are total opposites. She doesn't want a child but had one. Maybe that's why God put us together."

"What do you think His plan is for us? " Piper asked.

"His plan was for us to meet and to get to know one another. So far, so good, I must say." Monte smiled and took a sip of his coffee. He and Piper spent the next couple of hours getting to know one another.

"I would like for us to remain friends," Piper said.

Monte finished his coffee and asked Piper if she was ready to leave.

"It's been really nice talking to you, Monte."

"Good, I'm glad I could be of service, PJ. Would you like to meet my daughter one day?"

Piper took a second and thought it over. "Sure. When?"

"Harley has a dance recital on Saturday. You can join us if you're not busy."

"I'm looking forward to it, thank you," Piper said.

Monte paid the tab, left a tip for Daniel, and they left the coffee shop.

Piper tried to refresh her memory and recall a time when Monte had stared at her because of the scarf she was wearing to cover her increasing baldness. He had not mentioned anything to her about her appearance. Piper decided to break the tension and said, "It's still early. Do you want to meet my parents? Since we are at least going to be friends."

"Yeah, sure," Monte said.

As Piper opened the front door, she heard her mother rush from the kitchen window toward the door. "Piper!" she said. "Are you feeling all right?"

"Yes, I'm fine, Mom."

Piper motioned for Monte to come in. "Mom, Dad, this is Monte. Monte, these are my parents, Mr. and Mrs. Jackson.

Her parents looked shocked.

"Hello," Monte said as he shook Mr. Jackson's hand first, then Mrs. Jackson's.

"It's a pleasure to meet you, Monte," Mr. Jackson said.

"Yes, hello, Monte," Mrs. Jackson said. "Have a seat, son."

"Thank you," he replied.

Mr. Jackson launched into his regular routine of questions for anyone with an interest in one of his daughters.

"Did the two of you attend school together, Monte?"

"No, sir," Monte responded.

Mr. Jackson knew he could ask all his questions together but liked to draw them out. "The hospital?"

"Yes, sir. I'm a phlebotomist at the hospital."

"Have you ever been married?"

"Yes, I have. I'm divorced and a single dad."

"I see," Mr. Jackson said. Feeling a little uncomfortable now, Mr. Jackson said, "It was a pleasure meeting you." He stood, shook Monte's hand, and returned to the den to continue watching his program.

Mrs. Jackson could not take her eyes off Monte. It was as if she was reading his soul and trying to figure out his motives for her daughter.

"I'll leave the two of you to spend some time together," Mrs. Jackson said and returned to be with her husband.

"Maybe I should leave," Monte said.

"No, it's not you. They actually like you," Piper said.

"How can you tell?" Monte asked.

"You're still in the house. One thing you will realize about my family is that they are straightforward and will not bite their tongues. That includes my siblings."

"How many siblings?" he questioned.

"I have two sisters and two brothers. My sister Daphne is the eldest, then Brock Jr., Davon, and my sister Harmony is the youngest."

"I'm an only child, so I don't know what it's like to have siblings."

"Sharing!"

"Sharing?"

"Yes," Piper said. "We share everything except spouses."

"Well, that's good to know."

"We're a very close-knit family. What about your parents?" Piper asked.

"I never met my dad. He was killed at war. My mom lives with me. She helps me take care of Harley," Monte said.

"I'm sorry about your dad."

"It was a long time ago. I have pictures, but it's not the same. I don't know him," Monte said. He continued: "I better get going. It's getting late and Harley has school."

"Thanks for the conversation, Monte. It did make me feel better. I appreciate that," Piper said.

"You're welcome. I'll call you with the details of the recital."

"Great! I'll walk you out," Piper said.

They walked out to the street where Monte was parked. He asked, "Should we shake hands, or am I worth a kiss on the cheek?"

Piper turned her right cheek to Monte and said, "Put it there, friend."

He planted a long, passionate on her cheek. Too long and too passionate to be a cheek kiss. Piper didn't mind. She enjoyed every moment of it.

"Good night, PJ," Monte said.

Piper grabbed him by his chin, turned his face to hers, and said, "If your kisses get any better, I'm in trouble."

Monte took that as an opportunity to kiss her on the lips. He smiled and placed a nice, soft peck on her lips. "It gets better with time." He smiled.

Piper watched as Monte drove off.

When she returned to the house, she tried her best to avoid her parents, but her mother was at the door when she entered. "Piper, what do you know about this man?" her mother asked.

"I know he's a nice man," she said.

"He's also a married man, according to the tan line on his left finger."

"Mom! You noticed that?"

"Of course I did. And you should pay more attention to who you get involved with."

"Madeline! Let her be," Mr. Jackson yelled from his seat.

"Brock, you know I'm only looking out for her well-being."

"I'm grown and can take care of myself, Mom. And he's not married. He's divorced. I'm going to bed now," Piper left the room.

She did not want anyone criticizing her life, the one she would choose to live. If she wanted to date a married man, she would. If she wanted to kiss him on the first date, she would. Who did her mother think she was by spying on her and telling her who to date and who not to date? She should have said something about Scott.

After her scripture reading, she noticed a text message on her phone. She smiled, thinking it was Monte leaving her a message, thanking her for the evening, but was disappointed to see a number she did not recognize.

She hit the icon to read the message: *Hi Piper, I need to talk to you, to explain something to you that I should have explained a long time ago. It is not something I can do over the phone. It has to be in person. Can we meet tomorrow for lunch? Thanks Scott.*

Piper thought long and hard about how or if she should respond. Considering what she experienced with Monte today, she realized she didn't care anymore what Scott said or did. She did not care if he had a fiancée or not. She just did not care.

She smiled and started her reply: *I don't care anymore Scott, no need to speak to me about Darla. She told me everything and I do not care!*

She turned her cell off and smiled. She didn't want to know the details about Darla. She didn't want him to explain to her that this was the woman that ruined her marriage. She only wanted to dream. To dream about her future, with Monte. She smiled at the thought of becoming a stepmother. Then worry strutted across her face.

"Can I be a mother to someone else's child?" she thought.

Her tranquil night had been ruined by the thought of not being able to be someone's mother. Thanks to Scott.

She pulled the blankets over her head and tried her best to fall asleep.

Chapter Eighteen

When Scott returned from his business trip, he picked up a new cell phone to replace the one that Darla had kept. She told him she felt it was time Piper knew about her.

"Why didn't you tell me you were married, Scott? Does Piper know about me and the baby?" she cried.

"I'm not a bad guy, Darla!" he exclaimed. "I didn't mean to hurt you or her. I just could not tell her. It was just a mistake."

"I was a mistake or she was a mistake. You're not making this clear."

"Darla, let me tell her. I do not want you talking to her. Give me my phone," he demanded.

Darla had refused and kept his phone. She figured Piper had the right to know that she wasn't a homewrecker, that she was innocent. She didn't know they were married.

Scott had ruined the life of two women now: his first wife and his future wife. He never meant to hurt anyone.

Scott met Darla when he was on a drunken binge after an argument with Piper. Darla was tall, attractive and approachable — once his bartender friend Sebastian introduced them. He practically began seducing her at the bar and she had put up little, if any, resistance. After hours of dancing and drinking, Darla offered to drive him home because he was unable to do so. And because Scott was such a close friend to Sebastian, she felt that comfortable with him.

Instead, he asked her to take him to the nearest hotel so that he could sleep it off. Darla was a little tipsy herself and felt a nap was in order. She pulled into the local Hampton Inn and got a room with double beds. Scott made it in the door and dropped to the floor. Darla was unable to pick him up, so she left him there and covered him with a blanket. Then she flopped on the bed, exhausted.

When Scott awoke, he was a bit disoriented. He didn't know where he was or the woman who lay on the bed.

He made so much noise getting up that he woke her. "Who are you?" he asked.

"Darla. Remember?" Darla said.

"How did I get here? Did I drive?" Scott asked, confused.

"I drove. You were too drunk to drive, and I was just a little tipsy and needed to sleep. Do you remember anything about earlier tonight?"

"I wish I could remember you," he said, smiling.

That made Darla lose her smile. "Are you sober enough for me to take you to your car?"

"I'm sorry. I didn't mean anything by that. I just wish I could remember what we talked about," he explained.

He gathered himself. Got off the floor and sat next to Darla. "Look," he said. "I just had a bad fight with my girl and I think it's over between us. I went to the bar to clear my head. But now my head is clouded with the thought of you. You are simply beautiful, and I want to get to know you better."

Darla decided to relax. They talked for hours. Scott behaved like a gentleman.

"How about us having a late dinner?" Scott asked. He knew Piper was long asleep. His coming in late after a fight was normal.

The following day, he spoke to Darla over the phone for hours. They made plans for her to join him on his upcoming business trip. When they returned, Scott wanted to spend time with her every day. After a month or so of dating, she revealed to him that they were expecting.

Scott was elated — at first. Then he thought of Piper. How it would crush her. Scott had longed to be a father for years. He never got the courage to tell Piper, and her getting sick was the best excuse he could use to make a clean getaway. He would figure out later how to explain the baby. It was not that he didn't love Piper — he truly did. One mistake ruined what could have been.

Now Piper wouldn't speak to him. She refused to meet him and talk to him. How would he explain himself to Mr. Jackson? After getting his message, it would only be a matter of time before the truth would come out.

"Darla, please promise me you will let me tell Piper. I told you, she's ill. She has cancer, and I don't want to cause her any more grief than I already have," Scott asked of her.

"Scott, I don't know you anymore. Who are you? I'm not sure if I want a man that would walk out on me if I were ill."

"I did it *for you*. I never told you I was married because I wanted you. I wanted to be with you all the time. After we met, I couldn't sleep. I couldn't focus. You were all I thought about. My love for Piper had begun to fade. I want to be with you, Darla. I want our family. I truly am sorry about Piper, but I love you," Scott crooned.

Darla didn't know what to think, didn't know how to feel. She knew one thing and one thing only: She was not a homewrecker. She knew she had not known Scott was married, and she knew, as a woman, that she had to let Piper know as well.

"All right, Scott. I will not tell her. I'll let you tell her. But tell her the truth. I don't want her throwing eye daggers at me and my child if she sees us."

"Thank you, Darla."

Scott grabbed Darla gently around the waist. She hugged him in return. He kissed her gently on the neck and she gave in.

"I do love you, Scott. I only want us, as a family, to live in peace."

"We will, I promise." Scott said. "I need to meet with Mr. Jackson. He's disappointed that I haven't returned his call. I'll see if I can meet him for lunch in the evening."

"I want to go with you!" she exclaimed.

"Darla, please. This is something I need to do alone."

"Scott, there's something I haven't told you."

"What is it?" he asked as he pulled away from her, curious now.

"I've seen Mr. Jackson, and I spoke to Piper," she said bashfully. Ashamed.

"What?!" Scott shouted.

He took a seat on the nearest chair — he felt as if he would faint.

"When I had your phone, Mr. Jackson called and I answered. I didn't know what else to do. After speaking with him, I was determined to meet with Piper, so I went to her house. Hoping I could speak to her woman-to-woman, but there were people there. Moving her things. I parked down the street, but he saw me. He looked at me as I drove by. Honestly, I don't want to hurt her. I am not trying to cause her any undue grief. I just want her to know I am not at fault. I want her to know the truth," she exclaimed.

Scott held his head in his hands. "Darla, please, just let me handle this."

"There's more," she said. "I spoke to Piper, and I told her we were getting married," Darla said.

"You did what?!" he shouted.

"I just thought she should know. Why are you mad? We are getting married? Or have you change your mind?"

Scott stood and faced Darla. "There's no need for the insecurities, Darla. When I left Piper, I left for good, with no intentions of returning. Please, let me handle this. Promise me, no more calling her?"

"Yeah, sure. I won't call her," she said unconvincingly.

"I'm going to meet Mr. Jackson. I'll return soon."

"Sure."

He kissed her on the cheek and left.

She felt in her heart that Piper had the right to know. She had to hear it from her. Darla would wait. She would wait until the time was right and she would tell her. Tell her that she was not a homewrecker.

I wonder if I should take the baby with me? she thought with a fiendish grin.

Chapter Nineteen

Mr. Jackson watched as his daughter, Piper, wrapped the beautiful multicolored scarf around her head. She had not noticed him in the hallway with her. He walked up behind her as she stood in the mirror, watched as she did her hair dress. He offered to assist her.

"I'm fine, Daddy. I don't want pity," she said.

"It's not pity that I'm offering. It's a helping hand," he explained.

"I got it. It gets easier every day," she said.

Piper decided she was not going to dwell on the complications or side effects that her illness would bring to her life. Instead, she would embrace the hand that was dealt to her and deal with it the best she could. She would not accept pity. She would not let anyone bring her down. She was going to continue to live her life as if nothing was wrong.

Her father could not help but notice the change in his daughter's appearance. She was different. Her once long and luxurious hair was now short, brittle, and in patches.

"Have a big day today?" he asked.

"Yes, I'm going to Monte's daughter recital," she said.

"Well, have a great day," he said. He grabbed her shoulders with a fatherly touch and kissed her on the forehead. He left her to continue prepping.

The doorbell rang. It was Monte and his daughter.

"Piper, your ride is here," she heard her father say.

She looked in the mirror again. Took a selfie with all smiles to mark the day she met Monte's daughter.

Harley was cute in her yellow tutu and ballet shoes. She was all smiles when her dad introduced her to Piper.

"Hello, Harley, you may call me Ms. Piper."

"Hi, Ms. Piper. I like your scarf. It's pretty."

"Thank you," Piper replied.

"See you, Dad," Piper said as she and Monte left.

The recital was short. Sweet, seeing the little girls parade across the stage. One was a natural — she hit all the right moves. One just stood with her finger in her mouth, crying, wanting her mother to come and get her. Harley was cute. She danced and smiled. She was wonderful to watch.

When the recital ended, they went to BJ's for lunch. "I really enjoyed the recital, Monte. Thank you for the invitation. It was nice," Piper said.

"I'm glad you could attend. It's the first of many, I'm sure, that you will be invited to," he said.

"I look forward to it," she replied.

After lunch, Monte took Piper home.

Piper found her dad in the garage tinkering — basically doing nothing. Without turning around, he asked Piper how her day was.

"It was a great recital, Dad. I'm a little tired. I'm going in the house to take a nap."

She went inside and trotted up the stairs to her bedroom. Being home was like living in a five-star hotel. Her mom cleaned her room and changed her sheets regularly. She could always count on coming home to a freshly made bed. For that, she was grateful.

She didn't know where her energy had gone. She just knew she didn't have the strength for anything. As she lay waiting for sleep to come, she replayed the recital over again in her head. She realized that it wasn't just the children she wanted. It was the memories they would bring. She would remember this day for a very long time.

As slumber crept up on her, her cell phone buzzed. She was receiving a text message. The number again unfamiliar.

She read the text: *Hello, PJ. I need to speak to you, privately if possible. There is something I need to explain to you.*

"Explain?" Piper said aloud and continued reading.

Darla: *It's about Scott and our relationship. I think it is important for you to hear what I have to say. Please?*

Piper: *Scott? Who is this?*

Darla: *I'm his fiancée, Darla.*

Piper: *Let me be perfectly clear, Darla. Scott is your problem now. I do not care to hear anything you have to say about him. We have no ties. He's yours. And do me a favor? Please lose my number. Do not call or text me again.*

After Piper hit the Send button, she blocked the number.

Now I'll never get to sleep. Maybe I should have met with her, heard what she had to say. But do I care? No. I did the right thing. I do not need to know what her and Scott did or do. I really don't care. Piper thought.

She got out of bed to go downstairs for a warm glass of milk. That always put her to sleep. Before she could get to the door, her phone rang, but this time it was Harmony.

She answered the phone with much excitement. "Hey Harm!"

"Hey PJ. Are you busy?"

"No, just laying around."

"Okay, I'm on my way to get you to do a little retail therapy."

"Aw, Harm, I'm really tired right now. Can we do it tomorrow?"

"Sure, how about noon? We'll grab lunch and play catchup. Oh, and one more thing?"

"What?" Piper said, confused.

"I haven't forgotten about Monte."

Piper smiled and said, "I haven't forgotten either. I'll tell you all about him."

Piper slept all night. Her mother checked on her several times. Piper never budged.

She met up with Harmony later for lunch the following day. "So, who's Monte?" Harmony said before taking a bite of her veggie burger.

"We met at the hospital. He drew my blood the first time I went, before my chemo treatment."

"Was that all it took? Him to draw your blood?" Harmony asked.

"He told me that he knew all about me and watched me from afar for a long time. He's a nice guy. The night I texted you, we went and had coffee. I was feeling depressed about Scott and the divorce. He held a welcome ear. He's met Mom and Dad, too."

"Wow, he's met the parents?" Harmony said.

"I invited him in when we return from the café. He has a daughter name Harley. She's cute and very well-mannered. We went to his daughter's ballet recital as a first date."

"I'm happy for you, PJ. How's the treatment going?"

"So far, so good. I see the oncologist next week after my treatment. Let's talk about this wedding. You set a date?"

"Yes, May 22. The weather should be nice. We're planning to get married in church and then have a nice reception at Daphne's."

"Say what?" Piper said, confused.

"She said she would pay for the reception if we have it at her place. And you know Jason. He was all for it. Besides, it's a nice house and I'm sure she'll go above and beyond like she did for Savannah and Eric's wedding," Harmony said.

"I'm so happy for you, Harm." The sisters shared a hug.

"I decided to have an eclectic wedding. Nothing traditional. Everyone will be allowed to pick their own dresses within a particular color scheme," Harmony said.

"That's different," Piper said. "I think it will be beautiful."

"I chose my dress. It will be short and have a long, detachable train. Will it be white? I'm not sure about that," Harmony said.

"If not white, what color?"

"Cappuccino!"

"Oh, my. You're going Bohemian chic!" Piper said, chuckling.

"Yes, Bohemian chic. That best describes my wedding."

"I can do Bohemian!" Piper said.

"Are you done with lunch? Let's get in some shopping," Harmony suggested.

"Let's hit it!" Piper replied.

They strolled down the street, looking into jewelry stores, little boutiques and shoe stores.

"So, what is the color scheme for the bridesmaid dresses?" Piper asked.

Harmony pulled from her purse swatches of colors ranging from coco brown to beige. "I want earth tones. The groomsmen will wear tan-colored tuxedos. Jason just wants them to wear Jordan's Nike tennis shoes. I'm not sure about that. I rather they wear loafers. I'll convince him of it!" Harmony said.

Taking the fabrics in her hand, Piper touched, looked, and decided on her color: tan.

"Here, this is the color I want," Piper said.

"Great, I wanted you to have first choice. Now, I want you to choose a dress with bellow sleeves, short, right above the knee. The seamstress has the different patterns for all the dresses. There are many to choose from. I gave her copies of the swatches as well. We're going to have a meeting later next month to discuss who will wear what colors. I have time before the wedding, so now is the perfect time to get going on the dresses."

"So, who's in this wedding?" Piper asked.

"Besides you as my maid of honor, my best friend Megan is the matron of honor, and my bridesmaids will be Sabrina, and Carly from college, and Brittany. I would like Rena to be a junior bridesmaid. You know I have to have all my nieces. Savannah opted out, due to her pregnancy. I do need a flower girl. None of my friends have kids. Jason's nephew will be the ring bearer."

"Well, Monte's daughter is a cutie. She'll make a cute little flower girl," Piper said.

"Could you ask him?" Harmony asked.

"Sure. I was going to invite him to the wedding, anyway."

"Do you like him that much, PJ?"

"We decided that if we don't fall in love, we will always be friends. I think he really likes me, though."

"Cute," Harmony said.

"Well, if I get the spark, I'll ignite it."

"So, Scott. That's completely over? No feelings?" Harmony asked.

"They are dying, slowly but surely. A girl has texted and called me a couple of times, as if we were still in high school, claiming to be his fiancée. I don't care to know anything about them. I'm getting on with my life and I want him to do the same. She wanted to meet me, said she wanted to explain some things. I don't care to know, so I told her no-thank-you, in not so many words."

"Man, PJ. I would never have thought your relationship with him would come to this!"

"Right! I don't like to think about him, so let's change the subject. Are you ready to be a wife?"

They both laughed, took a picture on Piper's phone, and continued their shopping.

As Piper looked at the picture, she noticed something familiar in her appearance. Her features were altered. It wasn't quite noticeable to anyone else, but Piper knew. She knew all too well. She instantly got depressed and wanted to go home.

Chapter Twenty

Scott rang the doorbell to the Jacksons' home. This was a conversation he was dreading. Mr. Jackson knew about Darla and their son. He wanted to be the one to tell Piper that he was unfaithful, that he had begun a family. It was not that he didn't love Piper. He did. Very much. Just one bad decision, one night of passion, had altered his life, the one he shared with her.

In his eyes, Piper was the perfect woman. The fact that she couldn't have children made him rethink their relationship. Once Darla became pregnant, he knew he had to leave. He had planned to tell Piper that he was leaving, that he was unfaithful, and that she didn't deserve a lowlife like him. But her cancer diagnosis — that was his out. It was a coward's way out, but still an out. If it was not for his son, the one he had with Darla, he would have stayed, and he would have taken care of her. Now his bad decisions had led to this, his being labeled a cheater.

Mr. Jackson answered the door and ushered Scott into the den. "Let's make this quick. I'm not sure when Piper will return. Scott, this woman that you're seeing… What can I expect from her, as far as Piper is concerned?"

"Mr. Jackson, first let me apologize. I never meant to hurt PJ. I did something that I will regret for the rest of my life."

"Scott, you hurt my daughter deeply, and I don't want your friend causing her more pain," Mr. Jackson said is his deepest, most manly voice.

"Darla is harmless. She thinks she should be the one to talk to PJ, to let her know it wasn't her fault that our marriage didn't work out," Scott explained.

"I don't want that, Scott. You need to tell Piper, and you need to tell her everything. Soon. Or I will. I don't want this woman interrupting my family's peace," Mr. Jackson stated.

Scott nodded.

"Am I understood?" Mr. Jackson said firmly. "Keep this woman away from Piper."

"Yes, sir," Scott said, defeated.

"Thank you for stopping by."

Scott turned to exit the den. As he walked up the steps into the kitchen to leave through the back door, Piper walked through the front.

"Piper!" Scott said.

She knew the voice. She turned and shook her head.

"Can I talk to you?" Scott asked.

Mr. Jackson left the den and said, "I'll be in my bedroom if you need me."

Piper just stared at Scott. Her face said "what do you want?" She didn't need to open her mouth.

"How are you?" he asked.

She didn't speak, just shifted her weight to her other leg.

"Um, PJ, I am so sorry. I did not mean for any of this to happen. I did not mean for our life together to end this way. Please forgive me. I want to explain myself," Scott pleaded.

Without speaking, she again shifted her weight back to her other leg, as if to say "Speak!"

"Darla is a woman I met some time ago. I didn't plan anything. It was something that just happened."

Piper decided to sit, as she was getting nauseated.

"One night after an argument we had, I went to the bar and got drunk. I was too drunk to drive, and she offered to drive me home. I passed out before I could tell her where to take me, and we ended up in a position that I wish we hadn't."

Without speaking, Piper turned away from Scott. Her emotions overwhelmed her.

Finally, she said, "Is that it? Is that all? An affair? Now you're what, engaged to this woman? Is she pregnant? We haven't been divorced that long, Scott. Is that why you left? Because she's expecting?"

"No, PJ. She's not pregnant," Scott paused for what seemed like a lifetime, and finally said, "We have a son."

Piper jerked her head and stood at the same time. She wobbled and fell to the ground, knees first, then onto her side, and rolled over onto her back. Scott ran to her, said her name several times. She was unconscious. He yelled, "Mr. Jackson, it's Piper. She's passed out."

The thundering sound Mr. Jackson made running down the stairs startled Scott. He stood.

"Call 911. Now, Scott," Mr. Jackson yelled.

Scott obliged.

Mr. Jackson checked her pulse — her heart was beating. He called to her. "Piper, baby, wake up. Come on, Piper."

Bewildered, Scott didn't know what to think. He paced and ran to the door when he heard the approaching ambulance. The paramedics rushed through the front door, noted that she was breathing but not conscious. Mr. Jackson stood and let them do their job. He turned, noticed Scott in the corner, watching protectively as the paramedics tried to keep Piper alive.

"Scott? I need you to get it together. I will ride with Piper. Call the family."

Scott just stood as if no words were spoken. He watched the paramedics' every movement.

"SCOTT?" Mr. Jackson yelled. "I need you right now. Nothing matters but Piper right now. Call Brock Jr. I will call Madeline. Tell Brock Jr. to contact the family."

As the paramedics prepared to take Piper away, Scott yelled, "Where are you taking her?"

"Move, son," one said. "We're taking her to the nearest hospital, Palos Verdes General."

They asked Mr. Jackson several questions, which he answered. He told them she had cancer and was undergoing chemotherapy treatments. They transported her to the waiting ambulance and were off. Scott stood in the doorway until the ambulance was out of view. He was then reminded of the order Mr. Jackson had given him. He called Brock Jr. and gave him the news. Brock Jr. notified the family.

Piper regained consciousness in the ambulance before making it to the hospital. Mr. Jackson stayed with her in the back of the emergency room until the doctor finished his examination.

"Piper?" Mr. Jackson said.

"Yes?" she said.

"Do you remember what happen?" he asked.

"I remember talking to Scott, and I stood and got dizzy. That's what I remember."

"You're going to be fine."

"I feel so sick."

Mr. Jackson grabbed the yellow basin and held it under her chin as she vomited. When she finished, Mr. Jackson gave her a cup of water to rinse her mouth.

"What's wrong with me, Daddy?" Piper began to cry.

"We don't know, but we will find out. We're not leaving this place until we do." Mr. Jackson held his daughter in his arms and rocked her.

"Is Mom here?" she asked.

"The nurse said you had family in the waiting area. I'm sure she's there."

At that moment the emergency room doctor entered. He was tall and slender, with beefy hands.

"Mrs. Evans? How do you feel?" he asked.

"Sick," she said. "Am I okay?"

"We've run some preliminary tests and will have the results tomorrow. I've contacted your oncologist, Dr. Cheung, and informed him you were here in the hospital. He will stop by tomorrow. We're going to keep you for a couple of days to run tests to see what's going on. How have you been reacting to the chemotherapy treatments?"

"I get weak within a few hours. It's hard to keep food down, and I've had hair loss."

He took a miniature flashlight and looked into her eyes. "How long have you had this yellowing in your eyes?"

"I just noticed it earlier today," she said.

"Well, we'll know more once the test results come in. Dr. Cheung will give you the results."

"Thank you," Mr. Jackson said. "I'm going to check on the family. I'll be right back."

"Sure, Dad," Piper said.

Mr. Jackson entered the waiting room. Mrs. Jackson ran to him and asked, "How is she, Brock? How's Piper?"

"She's resting," he said.

Brock Jr. was seated next to his wife, Ashlyn, and Davon next to Renée. Harmony and Daphne were comforting one another. Scott stood off to the side, in a corner away from the family.

"What happened, Brock?" Mrs. Jackson asked.

"I'm not sure. She was fine when she walked in the house. Scott was there and they were talking."

"Did he upset her?" she asked with venom in her voice, looking at him with daggers in her eyes.

"It's not his fault. Something is going on with Piper. I can tell from what the doctor didn't say."

Mr. and Mrs. Jackson embraced. "I want to go see her," Mrs. Jackson said.

Mr. Jackson pulled away and ushered her to the room where Piper was resting, and then returned to wait with the rest of the family. "Scott?" Mr. Jackson said. "Come sit with the family."

Daphne looked at Scott with curious eyes. Harmony did not look at him, and Brock Jr. gave him a "nothing better happen to my sister" look.

Scott sat next to Mr. Jackson, as it seemed to be the safest place at the moment.

"You know this family, Scott. We don't do drama and we stick together. I know your relationship with Piper is finished, but Piper's well-being is our main concern. I don't want her under any undue stress, am I clear?" Mr. Jackson said.

"Yes, I understand. It's my fault that she's in here. I should have stayed with her, been there for her."

"The decision has been made. You can't undo what's been done," Mr. Jackson said. "We need to make the situation better. You need to tell this family what happened."

Scott spoke to the family, his head hung in shame. He told them about Darla. He told them about his son. He told them he was in the middle of telling Piper about the baby when she passed out.

Harmony looked at him in disgust, and so did Daphne. Brock Jr. and Davon looked at him as if they wanted to cause him pain for the pain he had caused their little sister.

"There will be no more discussion of this from anyone in this family. We are a family who trust and believe in God, and the one thing he teaches us is to be forgiving. The most important thing on this earth, right here and today, is Piper's well-being." Mr. Jackson looked at each individual member of his family as he spoke to them.

Brock Jr. and Davon stood and shook Scott's hand in forgiveness.

"She will have to stay in the hospital for a while until they find out what's wrong and how to treat her. We will have more information tomorrow when her test results come in," Mr. Jackson stated.

"Dad? Do you have her cell phone?" Harmony asked. "I need to contact someone and let them know."

Her father knew of whom she spoke: Piper's new friend, Monte. He reached in his pocket and handed the phone to Harmony. "Make the call outside," Mr. Jackson said.

Harmony took the phone and called Monte. She informed him that Piper had an incident and was in the hospital. He asked if it would be all right if he came to the hospital, and Harmony told him yes, she would like that.

When Harmony returned to the emergency room lobby, her mother had returned from visiting Piper. She told everyone that they were moving her to the sixth floor. The family would need to give them time to get her settled before they could visit.

"Scott, I think you should leave," Mrs. Jackson said.

"I want to make sure..." Scott began to say.

"LEAVE NOW," Mrs. Jackson yelled. "She told me what you said. You did this to her. It's because of you she's here and in this current state. Get out of my sight and stay away from my daughter." Tears streamed down her face.

Brock Jr. grabbed Scott by the shoulders and said, "I'll walk you out."

As they walked out the emergency room door, a tall man was running for his life into the emergency room. He nearly knocked Scott over as he ran through the double doors.

Chapter Twenty-One

Monte was out of breath when he reached Piper's family. He walked over to Mr. and Mrs. Jackson and asked about Piper.

"We'll be able to see her soon," Mr. Jackson responded.

Mr. Jackson introduced Monte to the rest of the family as Piper's friend. Davon shook his hand, Harmony gave him a hug and told him Piper had mentioned him to her, and Daphne said hello with skepticism.

"It's a pleasure to meet you all. How is she doing? Have the doctors said anything?"

"Who are you exactly?" Daphne asked.

"I'm a good friend of your sister, PJ. We met a while ago, and we work together."

"We don't know much — Monte, is it?" Mrs. Jackson said. "How much do you know about what Piper's been through?"

"I am aware of her illness. We spoke of it. I just want to make sure she's going to be all right."

"They're moving her to a room. It may be best if you return tomorrow. We are all going up when she's settled," Mrs. Jackson said.

"I understand. I just wanted to make sure she was all right," he said.

"She'll be fine," Mr. Jackson said. "I'll let her know that you checked in on her."

"Thank you, sir."

Harmony grabbed Monte by the hand and escorted him out of the emergency room. "She'll be fine. Don't worry, Monte. Come by tomorrow and see her. My family is just going through a rough patch right now and everyone is not themselves. I'll walk you to your car."

As they walked through the parking lot, they saw Brock Jr. arguing with Scott. "If anything bad happens to my sister, you will regret the day you married her and made us a part your life. You cheated on her, man. I want to beat some sense in you, but I don't think it would do any good," Brock Jr. said.

"Excuse me, Brock?" Harmony interrupted. "This is Monte, Piper's friend."

Scott looked Monte up and down and said, "I guess I wasn't the only one cheating, was I?"

Out of pure reflex, Brock raised his right hand, balled his fist, and hit Scott in the jaw. Scott fell to the ground, mouth full of blood.

Brock Jr. forgot that Harmony and Monte were standing behind them. He told Scott: "If you know what's best for you, you'll stay away from my sister."

Scott got up, wiped his mouth with the back of his hand, and walked to his car.

Brock Jr. turned to offer his apologies to Harmony and Monte. He shook Monte's hand, and gasped at the strength of Monte's grip.

"Scott deserved more than that," Harmony said and gave her brother a hug.

"Pleasure to meet you, Brock," Monte said.

"I was just walking Monte to his car. PJ should be in her room soon," Harmony said.

"I'm sure I'll see you again?" Brock Jr. questioned.

"If PJ allows it, then yes, you definitely will," he said.

Brock Jr. excused himself and returned to the emergency room.

"Thank you, Harmony, for being so nice to me. Will you keep me informed of Piper's condition?"

"Yes."

They exchanged numbers and said goodnight.

The lobby was empty when Harmony returned to the emergency room. She asked the desk nurse what room her sister was in and headed there to be with her family.

The Jacksons were all at Piper's bedside. Daphne held her hand.

"How do you feel?" Davon asked.

"I'm tired," she said.

"Has the doctor said anything?" Daphne asked.

"Dr. Cheung will let me know what's going on tomorrow. And I need you to promise — all of you to promise me — that no matter what he says, it will not alter our lives. And please do not show me any pity or treat me differently!"

"You will still be the same pain-in-the-butt little sister that you've always been," Davon said.

Her parents just looked at her as if she were the newborn they created many years ago. They were not going to make a promise they knew they would not be able to keep. They knew if it were bad news, they would not be able to not show her pity, to not pamper her. They would do everything in their power to make things better.

"Do you want us here with you when he tells you the outcome of your test?" Harmony asked.

"We will be here, Mom and I. We will hold a family meeting on Sunday and let the immediate family know what, if anything, is going on with Piper," Mr. Jackson stated.

Mrs. Jackson leaned over, kissed Piper on the forehead, and said, "I love you. Get some rest. We will see you tomorrow. Let's leave her to rest."

Everyone kissed Piper and said their farewells. Brock Jr. whispered in her ear, "I took care of Scott." He winked.

Davon said, "Get a good night's rest."

They left Piper to sleep.

Chapter Twenty-Two

First thing the following day, Dr. Cheung met with Piper.

"Hello, Piper. Are you feeling any better today?"

"Hello, Dr. Cheung. Yes, I'm feeling much better. What's wrong with me? Why did I pass out?"

"Piper, the cancer has spread beyond your breast. It's spread to your lungs, and the tumors are large."

Piper took a minute to let what he said settle into her spirit and into her soul. Once she realized the magnitude of what he said, she asked, "Okay, what's the plan? How do I get better?"

He sat beside her, held her hand, and said, "We have to fight. There is no cure for metastatic breast cancer, but it can be treated. We have to monitor the tumors that are in your lungs. You will have to be seen more often, to monitor the growth or reduction of the tumors."

Tears welled in Piper's eyes. The side effects were not enough pain for her. Scott leaving her to battle this alone was not enough pain. No, she had to fight. Fight for life. Fight not to die sooner, but later.

"If you feel up to it, you can be released today," Dr. Cheung said.

"How long do I have?" Piper asked.

"You can be released as soon as the nurse take your vitals," he stated.

"No," she said. She looked away, focusing on the gigantic oak tree that stood outside her hospital room window. "How long do I have to live?"

"Treatment of metastatic breast cancer focuses on length and quality of life. In your case, with proper treatment and quality of life, I believe you can live for a year or two, maybe longer. I am sorry, Piper, for this prognosis. Your cancer spread rapidly. And the only cases that I've worked with where it spread this rapidly lived for a year or two."

"Not your fault," Piper said. "It's God's plan. Is it all right if I take some time to think about it and talk to my family?" she asked.

"Of course. Call my office when you're ready. The sooner we get started, the sooner we can begin your treatments."

"Will do," Piper said.

After he left the room, Piper cried. She never thought about dying young. Now it was becoming a reality. She always planned everything in her life: her career, her wedding. She did nothing without a plan. *How do I plan to die? I'm not creating a bucket list, that's for sure,* she thought.

After the hour-long cry, Piper called her parents and informed them she was released. When the Jacksons arrived, Piper was sitting on the side of the bed, waiting for fresh clothes to put on.

"Do you want to shower here or at home?" her father asked, noticing her somber mood.

"Here. Mom, can you help me?"

Mrs. Jackson helped Piper into the shower. She dressed, got her paperwork, and left the hospital.

The drive home was quiet. She decided to tell her parents what the doctor said once they got home.

She sat with her parents, gave them the grim news. "I'm dying," she said plainly.

Her mom could not believe it. Her dad was beside himself.

"I never thought a child of mine would die before me," Mr. Jackson cried. "Has he said how much time you have?"

"He doesn't know. With metastatic breast cancer, there is no cure. The cancer has spread to my lungs."

Mrs. Jackson screamed: "No, No, NO," yelling louder with every word.

Mr. Jackson consoled his wife and sat her in the chair.

"I have to decide to continue with the chemo or not. If I continue the chemo treatments with a different medication, the side effects may be worse. Some women live for at least five years with treatment. It just depends."

"When will you begin the new treatment?" Mr. Jackson asked.

"I call for an appointment tomorrow."

"We're going with you, for support, to your next appointment," Mr. Jackson stated.

Piper knew she could not deter her parents from going. They had become her permanent caretakers.

"Dad, when you invite the family over, can you tell them? That will be too much for me to handle. I can talk to them individually, but can you tell them as a group?" Piper asked.

"However you want me to handle it I will," Mr. Jackson said.

"I'm exhausted. I'm going to lay down," Piper said.

Mr. Jackson helped his daughter up the stairs. She got winded halfway up and had to rest.

After putting Piper to bed, Mr. and Mrs. Jackson sat at the dining room table. "We need to move her to the bedroom downstairs," Mr. Jackson said.

Mrs. Jackson just cried. The thought of losing a child was inconceivable to her. She could not and would not accept it, not now. She could not.

Piper had no clue how long she could survive. She felt in her heart and soul that she was moving on. She looked and saw death in her eyes. Her cell phone rung and broke her daydream. She was not in the mood to talk to Monte. There was no use in leading him on. They did not have that fairytale dream waiting on them. She was dying and she could not have kids. *It's probably best that I not see him any longer,* she thought. She could avoid him — it was possible. She didn't necessarily have to have her lab work done at the same hospital. She could wait until she reached the center for her chemo treatments and have it drawn there. Harley would get over her. After all, they met only once. They had no ties. It would be easy letting him go. As soon as she thought those words, an ache filled her heart. She knew she was falling for Monte, and she felt safe and secure in his presence. She also knew she had nothing to offer him, not even the simplest thing: life. She was dying and she knew it. She just didn't know when.

Piper sent his call to voicemail to retrieve the message afterwards.

"Hello, PJ!" the message said. "I wanted to check on you, make sure you were feeling better. I'm not sure if you're still at the hospital. If so, I would like to stop by for a quick visit. Call me."

She could not and she would not call Monte. She didn't know how to let him down easy, so she did nothing. Nothing at all.

Chapter Twenty-Three

When Sunday dinner was done, Mr. Jackson sat with his children and gave them the news. The thought of losing a sister did not compute with Harmony. She just sat, stoic — didn't move, didn't speak, didn't cry. Even the boys cried. But not Harmony.

Piper offered to speak to each one individually and privately, with Daphne being the first. She knew she would be the most difficult one. She knew Daphne would put on her mother's hat and want to do motherly things and ask motherly questions. She really didn't feel up to it, but it was either deal with her now, or deal with her later.

As Daphne entered the room, Piper sat at her desk, reading about her disease online.

"Oh, PJ, you should be in bed," Daphne rushed to help her off the chair.

Piper withdrew. "No, Daphne, I'm fine. I'm not bedridden. I feel fine. I can still manage. I can walk and run and cook and do all the things you do."

"I was only trying to help," Daphne said, defeated.

"I'm sorry. I just want to be treated normal. I don't want special attention."

"Why not? You deserve it," Daphne said.

"Why do I deserve it, Daphne? Because I'm dying? Because I have a cancer with no cure? We are all dying — have been since the day we were born. Just some sooner than later."

Daphne cried.

"Don't start. Please, I can't handle this," Piper said and turned her back on Daphne.

"You don't have to be so cruel, PJ. I just want to help you."

"Daphne, please leave. And tell Mom that I can't do this tonight. We'll talk some other time. I love you, but I can't. Not tonight."

Daphne left the room. She relayed Piper's message to her parents, and no one else was allowed to see her.

Mr. Jackson took this opportunity to tell his family how strong they were as a unit. That no matter what happened, their family would prevail.

"Death is not the end of this family," Mr. Jackson said. "We are stronger than that. Death is natural. No matter how you look at it, we will all die from something. The most important thing I want from this family, and what I want you to relay to your families, is not to treat Piper any different. Let her be herself. No matter what she goes through, we will be there to support her."

Piper stayed in her room for days, only leaving to shower or to get a plate of food. Her mother would offer to bring her meals, but it seemed as if it was always when Piper was not hungry. She ignored Monte's calls. She felt no need to start something she could not finish. She would say to herself, "He wouldn't want to be with a woman that's dying, anyway."

But he was persistent. He called every day. Even tried reaching out to Harmony. He justified his calling by trying to get information on the wedding, but in reality, he just wanted to know how Piper was doing.

Harmony honored the bond she had with Piper. She never gave up any information. Monte was wasting his time. Harmony told him to give her time — she may come around.

Monte now felt as if he was intruding on family business, which was not his intent. He liked Piper, very much. Being with her was like winning a prize. When he found out she was divorced, he vowed to himself that, if she gave him the opportunity, he would love her unconditionally. He only wanted the chance to do that, to love her. Harley had a recital coming up. He had in mind to let her call and invite Piper. *She could not turn down a child, could she?* he thought.

After school, he asked Harley if she wanted to invite Ms. Piper to her recital and she was beyond thrilled. He allowed her to dial Piper's phone number. Monte knew if he called from his cell, she wouldn't answer. And he knew that after having left her several unreturned messages, she probably was not listening to them either. Harley called from his landline phone.

Piper's phone rang twice. The number was not familiar, so she ignored it and sent it to voicemail. She continued doing her research on her disease. *If it's important, they will leave a message*, she thought.

Later, she looked at her phone and saw that the caller had left a message. She retrieved it and heard the voice of an angel: *Hi, Ms. Piper, this is Harley. My daddy... Um, I wanted to invite you to my recital next weekend. It will be at the same dance studio at one o'clock. Please come.*

Piper knew Harley was being coached. Her speech was hesitant. She felt betrayed. Monte knew she did not want to see him, but she also knew how her heart fluttered when she saw little Harley dance across the stage. She could not disappoint her.

I will go to the recital. I'll take Harmony with me. I don't have to talk to Monte, or I can just say hi and keep it moving, she decided.

She tried calling Harmony several times, with no answer. On the final call, she left her a message asking to return her call.

It was almost a day later when Piper finally heard from Harmony. She had come to visit with her at their parents' house.

"What's going on, Harm? You have never not return my call immediately. Is everything all right?"

"PJ, this has got to be the hardest thing for me. I needed to get myself together before we spoke. You are my sister, my best friend, and I cannot imagine how you feel or what you are going through. I do not want to upset you. I just want to be there for you, whenever, however. And I don't want to make you cry."

"It is hard to accept, but I have accepted my fate. I just want you to continue to be my annoying little sister. I don't want things to change between us," Piper said.

The two shared an embrace and sat on the floor at the foot of Piper's bed.

"How are you feeling physically, PJ?"

"Okay, we are going to set some ground rules. Please, with all the love in my heart I have for you and the rest of the family, please do not ask me that anymore. I don't feel like a dying woman. It's just what is happening. I'm fine, Harmony, I am."

Harmony could not help but shed some tears for her sister, and before the next sentence, the two were in a storm of tears. Piper grabbed Harmony around her neck and said, "I'm not scared and I need you to not be scared for me."

Wiping the tears from her eyes, Harmony asked, "What do you need me to do for you?"

"Pray for me, for my soul, for our parents. Pray that our family get through this. Be strong for them," Piper said. "Let's make this our last cry. No matter what happens, let's not cry anymore? Okay?"

"I love you, PJ, and trying to imagine my life without you hurts."

"Then don't. Always remember the good and bad times we shared. I want you to take something of mine that would make you remember me and make you feel as if I'm around all the time."

Harmony scanned the room, taking inventory and trying to see what would always remind her of Piper.

Piper noticed and said, "Can you wait until the time comes? Please? I still want my stuff while I'm here."

The two of them laughed.

"The one thing I will take away from you, PJ, is your ability to always turn a bad situation into a good one."

"Speaking of bad situations, I need a favor," Piper said.

"Just ask and it's done," Harmony said.

"I need you to go to Harley's recital with me."

"Who's Harley?"

"Monte's," Piper said with a chuckle.

"Oh, sure, I guess if I want her to be in my wedding, I should spend some time with her."

"Thanks, but there is one thing," Piper said hesitantly. "I haven't spoken to Monte since the day I found out. I've been avoiding him."

"Why?" Harmony asked.

"He's a sweet guy and I think he deserves to meet someone he can build a relationship with, someone he could love."

"Do you like him?"

"I really do. I think we mesh well, but I don't want him to be hurt. He says he's had his eye on me for a long time, and I just think it's bad timing."

"What about Scott? How are you coping with that?"

With a faraway look in her eye, Piper tried to recall the last conversation she had with Scott, when he came to her parents' house and gave her the news. She tried to speak, "Scott's my cancer. I have nothing to say to him ever."

Chapter Twenty – Four

"Scott told me something the day I went to the hospital. He told me he has a son."

"We know." Harmony said in a whisper.

"Everyone knows?" Piper asked Harmony.

"He told everyone about his infidelities the night you went to the hospital," Harmony responded.

Piper was embarrassed. She felt the final break of her heart. There was no return. It was finally over.

"Do you know who she is, PJ?" Harmony asked.

"I'm not sure. She has my number and has called a few times."

"What? Scott gave her your number?" Harmony said angrily.

"I don't know. What I do know is, I do not want to waste any more time and energy on Scott. I'm ready to continue my life in peace."

"All right," Harmony said. "No more talk of Scott. Can we talk about Monte?"

"Why should I start something I can't finish? I don't see the use in calling and beginning a relationship when we all know how it will end," Piper stated.

"Give him a chance. I think you should at least return his call, PJ. When is this recital?" Harmony asked.

"Saturday," Piper said.

"Then just call and confirm our attendance," Harmony said.

Piper looked at her phone. It was not customary for her to be rude to anyone. She found Monte's number and dialed.

"Hello, PJ," Monte said. "I'm glad you called. How are you doing?"

Piper felt a sense of comfort in his voice. "I'm better. I got Harley's message. I would very much like to come to her recital, but I need to talk to you first."

Harmony took that as her cue and left Piper alone to speak to Monte.

"What did the doctor say? Are you going to be all right?"

Tears formed in Piper's eyes as she spoke. "Monte, I am very sick. I'm not well and I never will be."

An eternal silence. Neither of them spoke. Piper began to cry and so did Monte.

"Piper, no matter what, it's going to be fine. I want to be with you, to help you through this," he said.

"Why, Monte? Why do you want to be with me? Why do you care?"

"My heart has been full since we met," Monte said.

"Are you saying you love me? You don't know me. You know nothing about me."

"No, I don't know you that well. Can I say I love you? Maybe. I'm not even sure if it is love. What I do know is, you are a good person who does not deserve this part of life. I care about you. I want us to date, be friends," he confessed.

Piper let what he said sink into her heart. "Monte, I'm dying. There is no cure for what I have. The cancer has spread throughout my body."

"So, what are you going to do about it? Just take it or fight?" Monte said.

Piper was taken aback and said, "I — I'm going to fight."

"I'm going to fight *with* you. We may not have known each other long, but we can begin to know each other better. I want to spend as much time with you as possible. Can I stop by now? I really would like to see you," Monte said.

"How about I come to you?" Piper said.

"Are you up to it?" Monte asked.

"Is Harley around? I would like to see her."

"Yes, she would like to see you as well. She thinks you are so pretty."

"That's really sweet. Give me an hour to get myself together."

"Sure. I can't wait to see you. Piper, no matter what, I'm here for you."

"Thank you, Monte."

Mr. Jackson walked past Piper's bedroom door as she hung up.

"Piper, I need to speak with you."

"Coming, Dad," Piper replied.

Piper and her father walked down the stairs to the living area, the place where only serious matters were discussed.

"Have a seat," her father said.

Piper sat on the sofa nearest the door. She knew it would not belong before she had to leave to meet Monte, but she did not have the nerve to tell her father.

"There's something you need to know. I have spoken to the woman that is the mother of Scott's child. I tried my best to keep it from you. I have examined my conscience many times. How can I raise truthful children if I myself am not truthful with my children? I also spoke to Scott..." he began to say.

"When did you talk to her?" Piper said angrily. "Did you know he had come to tell me on that day?"

"Yes. I know you are angry. But so much was happening, and I apologize for keeping it from you for so long."

"SO LONG?! HOW LONG, father," she shouted.

Her father understood why she was angry, but he would never tolerate a child of his raising her voice at him.

"May I suggest you lower your tone and we can discuss this in a manner of *respect*," he said.

Piper had no more tears. She felt betrayed by her father. She could not look him in the eye. She lowered her eyes and said, "I apologize. But, Dad, how could you do this to me?"

"It was the evening you made your announcement. I saw them leaving the mall with a child."

Tears found Piper.

"Brock Jr. didn't think she knew the two of you were married when he spotted them in a restaurant," Mr. Jackson said.

"BROCK?! He spoke to her, too? I'm out of here," Piper said.

Piper went to get up from the sofa and her father politely said, "Keep your seat." She sat back down.

"Daddy, this is so unfair. What have I done to deserve a life like this?"

"You lived. Everyone has problems of all magnitudes. You, too, shall overcome this."

"When? When I die?" Piper said.

"If that's what God intended. He would never give you something you cannot bear. You are a strong black woman, and you deserve so much more than you are getting out of life. But this is your life and you need to figure out how to deal with it. You have your family. We are strong in our belief in God, and He makes no mistakes. Let Scott and this woman live their life. If he stays true to form, she will soon have to deal with other women, too. But let it go. Do not let it fester in your soul. Let it go, Piper. Forgive them," Mr. Jackson said.

Piper listened intently. She heard her father, she understood her father, but it did not stop her heart from aching. As far as she had been concerned, she was going to spend the rest of her life with Scott, her love, her best friend, her confidante. To know that this was not to be — It hurt and she could not fake it.

Her father gathered himself from his oversize chair and sat beside his daughter to comfort her.

"Did you see the baby?" Piper asked.

"Yes, it's Scott's. It's a boy. Looks just like him," her father said.

The confirmation eased the pain in her heart, slightly. "I want to see him," Piper said.

"Why?" her father asked.

"I need to see him so that I can be at rest. Will you ask Scott?"

"If that's your wish," he said.

Watching the grandfather clock in the corner of the living room, she realized she had to leave to meet Monte.

"I'm stepping out for a while and will return in few hours," she told her father.

Mr. Jackson held her hand between his and reaffirmed to her that what he did was to spare her any grief.

Piper kissed him on the cheek and said, "I'll be back."

She pulled her car from the curb and almost hit the BMW that had pulled alongside her. She didn't recognize the driver. She thought for a minute and could not figure out why she would not move her car. There was nothing stopping her from moving so that Piper could move her car.

Piper tapped her horn and motioned for the woman to move on. The woman responded by asking her to roll down her window.

Piper hit the button to roll down the window and said, "Yes, may I help you?"

Chapter Twenty-Five

Darla had decided it was time for Piper to know the truth. To know the truth and to know she had not planned to have Scott's child.

Scott's lies consumed her. She realized that he, in fact, did not live with his sister. It was Piper. The woman jogging to and from the house was Piper. She had wondered why she never saw his sister's kids or why he had never invited her over. It all added up now. Darla would park her car down the way from his so-called sister's house and watch the comings and goings.

Once the baby was born, Scott gave Darla a story that his sister had found a nanny, so he was no longer needed. Now he needed a place to stay. Darla wanted him to move in with her the moment they met. It was love at first sight for her, and she had not looked back since.

To Darla, Piper's outer appearance was that of conceit. Darla disliked women who were conceited about their appearance. She always felt she had something to prove to them. She was beautiful, came from a wealthy family and was intelligent and educated. She could hold her own in a conversation with anyone. Darla was more determined than ever to speak to Piper. Piper just had to know she did not break up her marriage.

Having friends at the DMV sure comes in handy, Darla thought as she set the navigation for the Jacksons' home. Her first mind was to get out, go to the door, and knock. She felt they would understand. The picturesque home was a two-story, beige colonial in a nice, suburban neighborhood.

She parked and watched for weeks the Jacksons' comings and goings and realized they were a large family. She tried calling Piper a couple of times to speak with her, to come face-to-face and talk about Scott and how their relationship had formed. It took weeks. When she finally got the nerve to speak, all she could mutter was, "Scott and I are engaged."

"What a dweeb," Darla said of herself.

Darla decided that she would accidently bump into her. Pretend to meet by happenstance. *Scott couldn't get angry about that, right?*

The day Scott returned home battered and bruised made Darla more determined than ever to speak to Piper. She did not buy that story that he fell down the stairs and got a fat lip. She began doubting anything Scott said, distrusting him.

The evening at Jacob's, when she thought he was going to propose, turned out to be about his status at the law firm. She agreed with him that it was an event worth celebrating, but she was disappointed it was not about her, their marriage, their family, moving forward, growing.

Piper's name was not allowed. She could not discuss anything about her to Scott, but she had to know. She needed details. She left Scott with the baby and pretended to go to yoga class.

She watched as Piper left her parents' house in a modern jogging suit, with a studded jean cap over her scarfed head.

"She looks different," Darla said aloud as if someone was sitting in her car with her. As Piper made her way to her car, Darla got close enough so that Piper could not pull out from the curb.

"Please, could you pull over? I need to speak to you. I'm Darla."

The shocked look on Piper's face said it all. Darla witnessed her expression change from confidence to curiosity. She wanted to know just what Darla had to say.

"Follow me to the coffee house around the corner. We can talk there," Piper said.

Anxiety enveloped Darla. *Now that I have the stage, what will I say?* Darla questioned herself. *I'll speak the truth. I'll just let her know that what happened was not intentional.*

Darla drove behind Piper's Lexus. They parked side-by-side in the coffee shop parking lot.

Piper extended her hand and said, "I'm Piper. Nice to meet you, Darla. Scott's fiancée?"

"Yes," Darla said with all the confidence in the world.

"Let's have a seat at the outside tables in the corner for privacy," Piper suggested.

"After you," Darla said.

"Why do you think we have anything to say to one another?" Piper began.

Stunned, Darla could not believe how aggressive Piper's tone was. She became frightened. Then she reminded herself that she was a woman who had approached another woman about cheating with her former husband. She may have had the same reaction.

"I'm sorry, Piper. Please just give me a few minutes to explain and speak about what has happened. I don't mean you any harm or distress."

"Oh, I'm not distress. I do not care anything about Scott or what he does. But, if it makes you happy, I will let you explain."

Darla told Piper how and when they met, how Scott never mentioned he was married. In fact, she always believed that Piper was his high school girlfriend.

Piper was not surprised. She had realized that she never really knew her husband, that she had married a total stranger.

Darla continued: "It wasn't until after we ran into your father at the mall that I found out he was married to you. By that time, we had just begun to live together, raising our son together."

Darla was surprised that Piper's expression did not change when she mentioned their son.

She continued: "If I had known he was married, I never would have pursued him. I am here to apologize for breaking up your marriage. For being the cause of all of this." Allowing her conscience get the best of her.

Piper was sympathetic. "It really takes a woman to apologize, and Darla, I do appreciate it, because it appears to be sincere. Thank you. But you were not the cause of our breakup," Piper said. "Scott was."

"I know it's mainly his fault, but I..."

Piper interjected: "Scott knew he was married. He should have never put himself in that position. Our relationship was strained because I could not have children, but I am happy now that he finally has a child of his own. I realized I married a total stranger." Piper thought for just a minute before telling her: "Darla?" Piper said. "I'm dying."

Chapter Twenty-Six

Darla was in shock. She wondered if this was Piper's plan to get Scott back.

Piper continued: "The evening Scott moved out from our home, I told him I had breast cancer. I was stunned by his comments, needless to say. That was when he decided to leave me, when I thought I needed him most. Now, you can take that information and do what you want with it. I want to live my final days in peace."

Darla tried to find deceit in Piper's eyes. What she found was truth and sorrow.

"Piper, I know many people who have survived breast cancer," Darla said.

"It's metastasized. I'm not sure how much time I have left, but what time I do have, I want it to be full of joy and with no regrets."

Darla thought long and hard. They sat in silence for minutes what seemed like hours.

Why is she telling me all this? I think she's sincere. I know it's not about Scott, but how could he do that to her? How could he leave her when she told him she was sick? Darla thought.

A crying child broke Darla's trance. "How could he leave you? Why?" she asked.

"He said that he didn't want to take care of me. I've gotten over it. I've forgiven him. I am mainly telling you this because I don't want drama in my life. I don't have time for it."

"Piper?" Darla began to cry. "I am so sorry for what I have done. If it weren't for me, Scott would have stayed. He would be here with you, taking care of you."

"Don't apologize for him. He did what he had to do. I hold no ill feelings against him nor you. I hope you guys are happy."

The sincerity in Piper's voice said it all. Darla looked at her in a different light. She wanted to know more about Piper, the woman dealt the bad hand in this life.

Darla asked questions. Not probing questions, but those of concern. "Does Scott know you're dying?"

"No, I don't think so. My brothers made him leave the hospital the night before I found out."

"Scott visited you in the hospital? See, he cares."

"He was at my parents' house when I had an episode. He came to tell me about his son. The past eight months of my life have been a nightmare. I get cancer, lose a husband and find out he has a child out of wedlock, and then to top it off, I'm incurable. Tell me, Darla, what would you do if that was to happen to you?"

Darla muttered, "I don't know. I honestly do not know. How do you keep it together?"

"My faith. This is what God has planned for me. Maybe on the other side, he has bigger plans. I have accepted my fate. I'm moving on with my life and I'm not letting anyone or anything keep me from being happy."

"Piper, you have such strength and strong faith. For you to sit here and communicate this to me, shows you are a remarkable woman. You're right. Scott doesn't deserve you. Nor does he deserve me. If he left you when you needed him most, what would he do to me? I have a son I have to be concerned about."

"Darla, I didn't give you that information to use against Scott. You are not me. Your life together may be different. Don't base the outcome of your relationship on what Scott and I went through."

"Sometimes, we women have to stick together. No matter what," Darla said with conviction. "May I hug you, Piper?"

"Sure."

They shared a hug and continued talking until Piper's phone buzzed. It was on silent so that their conversation wouldn't be interrupted. "Is everything all right? I thought you were on your way?" Monte asked.

"I got detained. I'll be there shortly." Piper replied.

Piper was so engaged in her conversation with Darla that she forgot her mission. After she hung up with Monte, she excused herself, wished Darla the best, and left.

CB&O

Darla was not expecting to feel the way she did. She had just witnessed the behavior of the strongest woman in the world. She was amazed at Piper's strength, her faith. She had no fear of death.

Her drive home was focused on the next conversation she would have with Scott. Playing through her head, over and over like a series rerun, was the scene of him telling Piper that he was not going to take care of her.

When she arrived home, she asked Scott if they could talk about a very sensitive matter. Curious, he suggested they go out to lunch and discuss what was on Darla's mind.

"We need to talk now. We need to talk about Piper," she said.

"I told you, Darla: I spoke to her. She knows about the baby. What else is there to discuss?"

"Why did you leave her?" Darla said with venom in her voice.

"I left to start a family with you, Darla. What's with the twenty questions about Piper?"

"You were never honest about her. You skated around your relationship with her and left her when she needed you most."

"Why are you so worried about PJ? It's over between her and..." Scott said, but was interrupted by his common sense. "You spoke with Piper? Darla, I told you I would handle it. You do not know her or her family as I do. I don't want you mixed up in all that."

"In all what? Her death? She's dying, Scott, and you left her when she needed you most. Would you leave me if I told you I had cancer? Would you, Scott?"

Twilight Zone. That's where Scott thought he was living. He did not understand — *could* not comprehend — what Darla was saying. "What are you talking about? Piper's fine, right?"

"No, Scott. The night she went to the hospital, she was told that the cancer had metastasized, and there is no cure for her," Darla said through full-blown tears. "How could you? I don't know who you are right now. I'm not sure if we're supposed to be together or not. Your place, right here, right now, should have been with Piper," Darla continued.

With a worried look on his face, Scott grabbed his keys and left the house.

Darla grabbed her cell phone and dialed the one person she knew she could count on in a crisis. "Hello, Daddy? I need to come back home."

Chapter Twenty-Seven

Monte was standing on the porch waiting for Piper to arrive. On her drive to his home, they spoke about her conversation with Darla. He could not wait to see her, to hold her and console her. When she locked her car, looked up and saw Monte waiting for her, she felt relief. She only wanted to hold him. She needed him to hold her and to tell her that everything would be all right.

"I feel you're the only person I can talk to right now," Piper said.

Monte held her and stroked her cheek and said, "I told you: I will be there for you in any capacity that you need me."

They entered Monte's immaculate home that he shared with his daughter, Harley, and his mother, Mrs. DuVal. The living area was open concept with modern furniture. On the mantle over the stone fireplace were portraits of three beautiful women. They were professionally dressed in one, and casually dressed in another. One had the three of them in swimsuits. Piper could not help but admire them. Their vibrant personalities shone through the photographs. She took a second glanced and noticed one that Monte heavily favored.

"Is that your mom?" she asked.

"Yes, and those are her sisters. They're very close."

"They're beautiful women," Piper said.

"Here, let's go to the family room and talk about what happened with your dad," Monte suggested.

"Apparently, my dad had a run-in with Darla and Scott the night I made my big announcement to my family — and didn't bother to mention it to me. I don't know, Monte. All of a sudden I feel as if I'm in this fight alone."

"Your father loves you and is looking out for your welfare," Monte said.

"If not telling me is in my best interest, then I don't think I have anyone on my side," Piper said.

Monte looked Piper in her eyes and said, "PJ, I know we haven't known each other long, but I feel strongly about you. I am what you deserve right now." He picked her hand up from her lap, placed a gentle peck on her lips, and said, "Piper, with my every being, I will take care of you. I do believe I'm falling in love with you and need you to take a leap of faith. Will you marry me?"

Piper turned and saw the sweetest petite diamond ring in Monte's hand.

"This is not what I was expecting" was all she managed to say. "Monte, I feel strongly for you, too, but to say yes, right here, right now? I just can't. I have to think about this. You have truly thrown me off my game." She had a brief thought. A smile crossed her face. She said, "I'm not saying no. I just want you to give me some time to think about your question. So I don't want to accept the ring just yet."

"Of course, it's understandable. Make sure your mom has the correct spelling of my name when she runs the background check." With that, they smiled.

"Where's Harley?" Piper asked.

"My mom took her to rehearsal and then to dinner. They should be here soon," he said.

"You have a beautiful home," Piper said.

"It's the home my dad grew up in, and when he died, his family gave it to my mom, and she in turn gave it to me so that it will stay in the family. She came to stay with me once Harley was born. It's been updated a few times."

"Very modern. You have great taste," Piper said, smiling.

"Mrs. DuVal, my mother, gets all the credit. She's the decorator. It has four bedrooms, a large den, and a swimming pool out back," Monte said.

"Can I take a tour?" Piper asked.

"Sure," he said.

They headed to the expansive kitchen and dining area that overlooked the family room. Portraits hung along the hallway wall. They appeared to be in some sort of chronological order, telling a story: A picture of a man and woman on the pier at a beach. Next, the two of them sharing a hug. Then a wedding portrait of the same two people. A photo of a pregnant woman and a soldier. The soldier on one knee kissing the pregnant woman's stomach.

"This is the story of how I became to be," Monte said, noticing Piper was spending a lot of time with each portrait. "My parents." He then pointed to the next photo and said, "From them came this bundle of joy." A portrait of a tiny, curly-haired infant with a distinctive smile. "Shortly after I was born, my father was killed in the military in a freak accident. The Army made sure my mother was taken care of for the rest of her life."

They entered a cute, pink bedroom next. Princess bed with matching dresser and a white desk for writing. "Harley's room?" Piper asked.

"Yes, she loves pink."

"Is this your room next to Harley's? Can I take a peek?"

"It's my mom's room. She dotes on Harley and wanted to be close to her. Mine is down here."

Down the hall in the back of the house was a large master bedroom. Monte opened the double doors that led them inside. Piper could not help but say her first thought: "I can live like this!"

The California king bed was the center of attention. The bedding décor was black and gold. The fireplace resembled the one in the family room. Dressers lined the walls on one side of the room and on the other side, an entertainment center. The master bathroom was massive. The cast iron freestanding tub caught Piper's eye. The spa-like shower was decorated with different shades of gray tile and fit for a queen.

"Walk-in closet?" Piper said as she pointed to the double doors on the side of the master bathroom.

She opened the doors and was amazed at the size of the closet — and how organized it was. "Your mom gave this up to be next to Harley? I could live in this room," she said.

Piper began a mental reorganization of Monte's things to include her belongings in the endless closet. There was definitely enough room for her and all her things. When she turned to walk out of the closet, a broad smile lit Monte's face. "So, what do you think?" he asked.

"This is really nice, Monte. I just may say yes for the closet alone," Piper said, laughing.

"Well, you know that would be a package deal: the closet and me," he said.

Piper hung her head. This was the first time he had seen her like this. "Monte, I wouldn't make you a good wife, or be a good mother to Harley. What could I do for you? I'm not even sure how much longer I will be around."

With sincerity in his heart and voice, Monte plainly stated, "I don't care. I love you enough right now to spend our final days together. I could be hit by a car tomorrow, die and leave you alone. Life is not a luxury that people can take their time with. Do what you can, when you can. Life is not a promise for the next day. All I ask is to give me the chance to make your life a happy one."

Piper thought about the words "make your life a happy one" and said, "This is not something I will take lightly. I will definitely consider it, but may I ask you one question?"

"Yes, Ms. PJ," he answered.

"Why me?"

Chapter Twenty-Eight

Scott was furious that Darla would go behind his back and talk to Piper. *I asked her not to do that*, he thought as he drove to the Jacksons' home.

Once he pulled up, he saw the entire family's cars parked out front: Brock Jr., Harmony, Daphne, and Davon. Something big was happening. He jumped out of the car and ran to the front door. He tried to open it, but it was locked. He rang the doorbell, one ring after another, until someone answered. "Scott, have you lost your mind, young man?" Mr. Jackson said.

"What's wrong? Where's PJ?" Scott said with an urgency in his voice.

"Come in. Have a seat," Mr. Jackson offered.

"Where is she?" Scott yelled.

"Come in and have a seat," Mr. Jackson said again.

Scott entered the Jacksons' home. Everyone was in the family room having dinner.

"Would you like something to eat?" Daphne offered sarcastically.

"Mr. Jackson, where is PJ? I need to speak to her."

"She left yesterday, and I haven't heard from her."

Scott lowered his head and said, "she met with Darla yesterday."

Everyone was silent for what seemed like an eternity.

"Scott, this is all your fault," Mrs. Jackson said.

"I do apologize for what problems I may have caused, but with all due respect, I'm not responsible for her not being here, right now. I haven't spoken to Piper since the day she took ill," Scott said.

Brock Jr. walked over to Scott, Davon in tow. "You are responsible for her being there in the first place. Don't turn this on my sister," Brock Jr. said. Davon echoed it.

"Brock, Davon, respect my home," Mr. Jackson said before things escalated.

"I need to speak to Piper. Mr. Jackson, how sick is she?"

"She's..." Mr. Jackson began to say but was interrupted by Mrs. Jackson screaming.

Mr. Jackson turned to console his wife. Davon put his hand on Scott's shoulder and escorted him to the front door. "I think it's time for you to go, Scott. You need to leave and since you didn't want to be a part of this family, stay away from it, you understand?" Davon said as they reached the front porch.

Scott got in his car and drove off. He had nowhere to go. The person he would turn to was no longer there for him. He needed Piper. He wanted to hold her and apologize. He didn't mean what he had said to her. He didn't want to leave her. He only wanted time with his son. He never imagined his life without her. Even with the divorce, he knew she was the one person he could count on at any time, who would always be there for him.

"Where is she?" Scott yelled to himself.

He drove and drove. He thought of all the places she could be. He drove past the coffee shop they frequented. He phoned her closest friend. No luck. Then he remembered the one place she would go when she wanted time to think about life.

He drove his car down the 101-freeway heading toward Santa Barbara. Piper found solitude in staying at the Cheshire Inn. The beach and the waves calmed her.

After hours of driving, he realized that his cell phone had not rung the whole time. He knew Darla was probably somewhere crying her eyes out. But right now, Piper was his main concern.

As he pulled into the hotel parking lot, he noticed Piper's Lexus and sighed with relief. It was the afternoon and the sky was overcast. It was too cold, so she was probably not by the beach. He knew he would have to wait her out, wait for her to leave her room. He decided to walk to the nearby café and get a cup of coffee.

As he opened the door, a woman in the first set of seats was sitting with a man that Scott recognized but could not place. From behind, the woman resembled Piper. Then it came to him that it was the man from the hospital. He had to make a quick decision: Did he want to hide and just watch them? Or did he want to approach and question this man with his ex-wife?

Scott approached the couple and said, "Hello, PJ."

Piper was stunned. Scott was the last person she expected to meet in Santa Barbara.

Monte stood and greeted Scott. "Hello. We didn't officially meet last time, but I'm Monte, a friend of PJ's. And you're Scott, correct?"

"Yeah, her husband."

"Scott, don't start. Monte knows we're divorced. Why are you here? Is Darla with you?" Piper said.

"No. I need to speak to you, PJ," Scott said.

"We have nothing to discuss. If you want to sit and have a cup of coffee, you are more than welcome to do so," Piper said as she showed him the seat next to Monte.

Scott took a seat and just stared at Piper. "Is it true, PJ?" he asked.

Knowing exactly what he was talking about, she shook her head yes. "Scott, I have forgiven you for what you've done, so let's just keep this amicable and say goodbye now," Piper suggested.

Scott was bewildered. He didn't know what to say. Stunned by her comments, he had not noticed the tears that flowed from his eyes. Monte handed him a napkin. Scott accepted.

Piper continued: "I know Darla has told you about our conversation, so if you don't mind, I'd like to get back to my conversation with Monte. My fiancé."

Monte was just as surprised as Scott.

Scott stood and looked from one to the other. "Fiancé? PJ, we haven't been divorced that long," Scott cried.

"How old is your son? I know I don't have children, but it does take at least nine months before they're born, and he's what? Six months old? Let's do the math: six plus nine is fifteen months, and there are only twelve months in a year. So, if you can do it in under a year, so can I. Yes, Monte, I will marry you!" Piper said.

"Piper, I will not allow you to disrespect me like this, to my face!" Scott replied.

At that moment, Monte stood and suggested to Scott that he should leave not only their table, but the café. "Let's talk outside for a moment, Scott," he said.

Piper turned her head so that she wouldn't witness what happened next.

"Mr. Evans, please. Let's not cause a scene. Let's go and have a gentlemen's conversation outside," Monte said.

Scott noticed the seriousness of Monte's face. But he wasn't getting any help from Piper, so he decided to go with Monte.

"You know, Monte, it won't last. Piper will come back to me. I am her first and only love. So, you can have your fun with her for now. She'll get bored and return to me, especially when things get tough," Scott said.

"Is that right?" Monte asked sarcastically. "Well, let me say this: Now that Piper and I will be together, I will let nothing and no one hurt her. Ever. And that's including you. So, I will do what I have to do to protect her, and just because we haven't known each other that long — It doesn't mean a thing to me. I love her and will continue to love her." Monte took a couple steps closer to get in Scott's face. "I don't go for bad, but I do protect my family. You stay away from *my* future wife. If you cause her just one millisecond of pain, I will cause you pain. And I mean that."

Monte walked away.

Chapter Twenty-Nine

Monte walked back into the café. He couldn't help but notice the tears in Piper's eyes. "Just when I thought I knew what I wanted out of life, I..."

Monte interrupted, "Piper, I know this has your feelings all twisted and it's okay. I know what you said was out of anger with Scott."

"But it wasn't. Monte, my last doctor's visit since I left the hospital was depressing. I don't know if I'll be here tomorrow or five years from now. I'm not critical now, but who knows when I'll become that way. I don't want my parents to worry over me. My faith in God is strong. But I would be lying if I said I wasn't scared."

Holding Piper's hand, Monte said, "It's only natural to be scared. But I will be here for you, Piper. Remember you asked me 'why you?' You wear your heart on your sleeve. You walk with such confidence, and I love you very much."

Piper put her head on the table and finished her cry, and Monte held her hand.

"I do like you — a lot — and if given the chance, I know the strong like will soon be love. You will just have to be patient. I'm going back to my family's house tonight. Thank you for staying with me last night. I couldn't face my dad after the other day," Piper said.

"I'll follow you home and call you later," Monte said.

"Thanks for being the perfect gentleman last night. You didn't have to come with me."

"Yes, I did. I couldn't have you coming to a hotel alone when you've gone through so much. We'll talk later, maybe have dinner after you sit and talk to your family."

They shared a kiss, embraced each other, and went to their respective cars.

Monte could not contain himself. Just being alone in the room with Piper had him convinced that this was the right thing to do. After about five miles, Piper exited the freeway, still in Santa Barbara. She drove west, toward the beach, and Monte followed.

She parked and got out of the car.

The air was cold. No sun. She looked across the still water. Monte approached slowly behind her. "Is everything all right, Piper?"

"I want to get married here, on the beach," she said.

Monte came closer and said, "Anything you want."

"I love the beach. It gives me peace. Will you sit here in the sand with me?" Piper asked.

"Sure, let me grab us a couple of jackets," Monte replied.

They sat in an embrace until the sun began to set. The conversation was minimal.

"I think we should go. Your family must be worried," Monte said.

They stood and wiped the sand from their clothes. They shared another kiss and continued their journey home.

When Piper arrived at her parents' home, it was dark and still. It had the same eerie feeling it had when she had missed curfew in high school. She opened the door to find her father sitting in the same spot he had been when she left, now in the dark.

She went to turn on the lights and found him in tears. Her father was a strong man, a hardworking man who had taken care of his family. To see him in this state bothered Piper.

"Daddy, I'm sorry I left the way I did," she said.

"Have a seat near me, Piper," he said.

She set her belongings on the table and sat next to her father.

With his arm tight around her, he said, "Your mother was worried. You should have called her. I insisted that she go to bed early." He took a tissue from the box on the table and dried his face.

"I'm sorry I caused you guys to worry," Piper said.

"Piper, I cried tonight because I know my life will be changed profoundly by not talking to you or seeing you on a regular basis. This affects the entire family. I know that life sometime is not fair, and you may feel like your life is being cut short, but God has a plan for us all."

"Daddy, I have come to terms with my situation. I love God, and I know He doesn't make mistakes. I just want to be happy with what time I have left. I am going to marry Monte."

Mr. Jackson looked confused. He had to recall the name of the gentleman he met in the hospital. "How well do you know him, Piper?"

"Dad, please. I know that he cares for me enough to take care of me when I get sick — something my former husband didn't want to do," she said.

Again choosing his words wisely, Mr. Jackson took his time responding. "When do you plan to do this?"

"As soon as possible. I don't want to wait."

"Do you love him, Piper?" he asked.

"I really do care about him," she said.

"All right. Tell me about him."

She told him all she knew about Monte. She told him his father had died in the war, that he was raised by his mother, alone and about the crush he had had on her for years. Mr. Jackson decided that if Monte were going to join the family, they would need to speak.

"Let's have a surprise wedding here, at the house. A small gathering, just family, ours and his," her father suggested.

"Really?"

"Yes, why not. The family will be shocked and happy. I'll take you and Monte to dinner tomorrow and we'll make the arrangements."

"Oh, boy, will Daphne be mad at you," Piper said, laughing. Her father joined in. "Do you mind if I wake Mom to apologize?"

"No, go ahead. She'll be happy to see you. But remember, it's a secret."

"We're not telling Mom either?" she said, curious.

"No, that will be just like telling Daphne, and that would be like telling everyone in the family, and there goes the surprise."

"Boy, you are really asking for trouble, Daddy."

⊂⊃

The gentle knock on the door woke Mrs. Jackson. "Come in," she said.

"Mom?"

"Oh, Piper, are you all right?" Mrs. Jackson asked. She leaped from the bed and embraced her daughter.

"I'm fine, Mom. Just needed some time to think."

"Piper, you know you can talk to me about anything, right?"

"Yes, I know."

Her mother gave her another hug and kissed her on the cheek. "Next time, just let us know you won't be home. I was worried sick."

"I will, Mom. Goodnight. I'm going to shower and go to bed."

"All right, sweetheart. And remember, if you need to talk, or need someone to help you with anything, I'm here."

"Thanks, Mom."

She went to her room and noticed that she had a missed call from Monte. She returned it only for it to go to voicemail. She left a message telling him they had a dinner date with her dad.

After her nightly routine, Piper checked her phone and found a text message from Monte. It was an emoji biting his fingernails. Piper laughed and went to bed.

Chapter Thirty

Scott entered an empty house. *Now what?* he asked himself. He reached for his cell phone to call Darla. No answer.

He sat on the floor and thought about the last few months. Decisions he made that had affected everyone. How disappointed his mother would be for treating Piper the way he did. She admired and loved Piper like a daughter. They had a special relationship. He remembered his mother's final words to him: "Son, be respectful to Piper. Treat her like you would me, but only better."

Tears formed and flowed from Scott's eyes. He thought about the deceit and the lies he told Piper. The night Piper told him about her illness, he thought that was the perfect opportunity to leave and be with his son. He never thought it would come to her death. *Her sister had survived cancer. Why not Piper?* he thought.

He did care about and love Darla, but his heart was with Piper and her every being. He was conflicted between his son and Piper. He loved him more. For him to be with his son, he had to be a part of his upbringing. He just didn't know any other way to express his feelings to Piper. He thought if he gave it time, she would forgive him and accept his son. But he needed time.

A text message broke his trance. Darla had responded via text instead of returning his call. *Scott, I can't right now. Please give me time.*

What the hell Darla? Where's all the stuff? When are you coming back home? Scott replied.

Darla: *I don't know if I want to come back.*

Scott thought long and hard before responding. Now that Piper didn't want him anymore, he needed to make amends with Darla.

Scott: *I'll give you all the time in the world. I am sorry Darla. For everything.*

Darla: *We'll talk later.*

Scott felt his life spiraling out of control. He needed his mother but knew she could only hear him in his dreams.

He needed to talk to a levelheaded person who would understand. Scott thought that if Piper would not talk to him, maybe Harmony would.

◦₃◊₀

Harmony was shocked when Scott wanted to meet with her and talk. She didn't know what to expect. She wanted to talk to Piper first, to see if she had any insight.

"What's up, Harm?" Piper asked.

"Did you speak to Scott?" Harmony asked.

With a curious eye, Piper asked, "Why? What did you hear?"

"Nothing. He called me and wanted to talk. But I would never talk to him before finding out what's going on."

Piper closed the door to her bedroom. "Can you keep a secret?"

"Of course. What's up?" Harmony asked.

"This is a Daddy secret," Piper said.

"That means a double pinky promise," Harmony replied. They hooked the pinkies of both hands together.

"Daddy is going to have a surprise wedding for me, here at the house, and he said tell NO ONE!" Piper exclaimed.

Looking confused, Harmony responded, "I don't understand. Why did you and Scott get divorce, just to marry again?"

"I'm marring Monte," Piper said confidently.

"Monte?" Harmony said. "You barely know him. He's cute and all, but what about the rest?"

"He loves me. Has for a while, so he says. He wants to take care of me."

"Does he know everything?" Harmony asked.

"Yes, he does. He wants my days, no matter how many I have left, to be filled with love."

Harmony hugged Piper.

"Harm, you can't tell anyone about this," Piper said.

"So, when's the big day?"

"Daddy wants to take Monte and I to dinner to discuss the particulars," Piper said.

"I want nothing but the best for you, PJ. And make sure you tell Monte that we are a package deal."

"You know it!" Piper said.

"So, what's the plan?" Harmony asked.

"I wanted it at the beach, but Daddy said it would be nice to have it here. In the backyard."

"Ooh. Daddy is going to be in trouble. Having a party and not telling Mom so she can have the cleaners come in and clean this place from top to bottom."

Piper thought for a second and said, "You're right. I'll remind him of that."

After debating whether or not to leave, Harmony suddenly remembered why she was there. "So, do you think Scott knows, and that's why he may want to talk to me?" Harmony asked.

"Oh, he knows. I spent the evening in Santa Barbara with Monte. And..."

"What?" Harmony interrupted.

"It was platonic. I needed to go and clear my head, and he didn't want me going alone after meeting with Darla, Scott's fiancée."

"WHAT?" Harmony yelled. "You met with her?"

"It's cool. We had an amicable conversation. She apologized for getting involved with Scott. She said she had no idea Scott was married. She sound sincere, but I really don't care."

Harmony went to Piper and suggested they sit on the bed. "PJ, I am so sorry I haven't been here for you lately. I was being selfish, only thinking about how I feel," Harmony cried.

"It's all right. I know it's hard. Besides, you are planning a wedding. And no matter what happens, I will be there for you. If I can, I will stand by you," Piper said.

"I love you, sister," Harmony said. "Now, what should I do about Scott?"

Piper said, "Whatever. I don't care anymore."

"I guess I'll have him stop by the house when I return home. You want me to call you afterwards?"

"Nope. Not interested. I feel like I am getting something new with Monte, and I don't want to include Scott or his name in any of it."

They said their goodbyes and Harmony left the house.

"Daddy wants us to go to dinner tomorrow." Piper said.

"Aw, Piper. Harley has a recital tomorrow evening. Can we make it lunch?"

"That's perfect. That way he can meet her as well. I'll meet you guys tomorrow at the dance hall."

"All right, it's a date. Should I be nervous? If not, I am!" Monte exclaimed.

"Just think, in a few weeks, you will have a new wife," Piper said.

"I won't let you down, Piper. I promise," Monte said.

"Pinky promise?" she asked.

"Yes, pinky promise."

Chapter Thirty-One

It was midnight when Scott finally returned Harmony's phone call. *Intoxicated* was an understatement. Scott was flat-out drunk. He slurred his words so badly that she couldn't understand him. She hung up on him, rolled over in bed, and went back to sleep.

Scott returned to his empty condominium and after an hour of vomiting, he sobered up.

"I need to get myself together," he said. He went into their old bedroom and luckily, all of his clothes were still there. He showered with only hot water, as there was no soap.

Scott needed to make amends today with Darla. His mother had told him it was time.

He spoke with Darla, and they decided to go out to lunch, alone, without the baby.

Jacob's was their favorite place. It is where they had their first dinner, so they met there in separate cars.

"Hello, Darla," Scott said and greeted her with a kiss. "I know I made a mess of everyone's life, especially yours. I was wrong not to tell you I was married. I was wrong not to stay with Piper when I found out she was sick. I was just wrong. I ruined so many lives."

"And how did you come to this conclusion, Scott?" Darla asked.

"My mother," he said, lowering his head.

Knowing his mother had died some time ago, she said, "Come again?"

"I wanted to talk to Piper's sister but she was unavailable, so I went to the bar. The bar where we met. I drank until I was nearly in a coma. I thought about you, and I thought about Piper. Then my mom came to me as if she was sitting right next to me and she said: 'Son, no matter what, I am proud of you. We all make mistakes in life. It is learning from them that makes you a better person. You can't change what has been done, but you can make things right. I love you, Scott.' My mom and I were really close. I would talk to her whenever I had a problem with anything, and she would always give me her honest feedback," Scott said.

Darla looked through the tears in her eyes and said, "So, what does all this mean, Scott?"

"I'm going to apologize again to the Jackson family, for the mess I made. And..." Scott got down on one knee in front of Darla and said, "Darla, I'm not perfect, but I'll make you and God a promise: I will be the best husband and father that I can be. I will provide for you, through sickness and health. I love you, Darla. Will you please marry me?"

Darla could not contain herself. She fell in love with Scott all over again. She grabbed his face with both hands and kissed him softly on the lips.

"Yes, Scott, I will marry you."

They kissed long and hard as if no one else was in the room.

The maître d' interrupted with, "Excuse me, but may I take your drink order?"

They smiled, took their seats, and ordered a bottle of Cristal to celebrate.

They continued the evening discussing wedding plans. Venues, colors, and food. This would be the first wedding for Darla and, being that she came from a wealthy family, it would be extravagant.

During dessert, Darla had suggested that Scott call Mr. Jackson and meet him tonight in public, to apologize. Mr. Jackson accepted.

They met at the café near the Jacksons' home for coffee. After ordering a cup, launched into his apology. "Mr. Jackson, first let me apologize for making a mockery out of my marriage to Piper. I apologize for hurting Piper and your family."

"Apology accepted," Mr. Jackson said firmly.

"I would like to apologize as well, Mr. Jackson," Darla said. "I didn't mean to cause any problems for anyone."

"Accepted. I will inform the family of your apology. But Scott, I think you need to apologize to Piper face-to-face, as well as to my wife."

"I would, but Piper won't talk to me," he said.

"I'll speak with her and let her know your intentions. I'm sure she will come around."

"Thank you, Mr. Jackson," he said.

The ding of the bell over the door caused everyone to turn their heads. Brock Jr. and Davon entered. They knew their father was there meeting with Scott and decided to show up.

"Dad, everything all right?" Davon asked.

"What, you think I can't handle Scott, if need be? What are you guys doing here?" Mr. Jackson asked.

"Well, Mom said you were meeting with Scott, and...", Brock Jr. started.

"And what? You think he wanted the jump on me, and that I needed the two of you for backup?" Mr. Jackson laughed a hearty laugh like he hadn't laughed in months.

"I met him here so that we could apologize to your family for causing such a mess." Scott stood and held his hand out to shake Brock Jr.'s.

"Apology accepted," Brock Jr. said.

He did the same with Davon.

"What's going on here?" a familiar voice asked from behind Davon. Mrs. Jackson had made her way to the café as well. "Brock Sr., what is this all about?"

Scott reached over to give her a hug and apologized, but she rejected the gesture. "Scott, what is it?" she said.

"Mrs. Jackson, hurting Piper was the farthest thing from my mind. I never meant to hurt her. I made a mess out of everything, and I apologize from the bottom of my heart to you and your family."

With her nose mounted in the air, Mrs. Jackson looked around the café, fixing her eyes on Darla. She looked her up and down as if she were reading a vertical sign.

Scott motioned for Darla to stand next to him. He introduced her to Mrs. Jackson as his fiancée. Darla extended her hand to shake Mrs. Jackson's hand. She reciprocated. "Married so soon Scott?" Mrs. Jackson asked.

"I made a mess of things, I know that, but I'm trying to make things better. I had a child out of wedlock with this woman here, who was totally innocent. She didn't know I was married, but it is what it is. Piper has moved on from me. She's engaged to Monte now, so I feel it's time for me to move on as well."

No sooner had the word "engaged" exited Scott's mouth than Mr. Jackson covered his face with his hand.

"What are you talking about, engaged? Piper don't have time for that," Mrs. Jackson said.

Everyone noticed that Mr. Jackson was not saying anything. He had a broad smile across his face.

"Brock?" Mrs. Jackson said to her husband.

"Dad?" Davon and Brock Jr. said in unison.

"Well, the cat's out of the bag now!" Mr. Jackson said.

Chapter Thirty-Two

"How could you try to plan something at our home without involving me, Brock?" Mrs. Jackson said.

Mr. Jackson had no choice but to tell them about Piper's plan to marry Monte. Mrs. Jackson was not receptive to the idea at first, but she came around when he told her what Piper had said: "Her last chance at love."

The dinner went well. Everyone treated Monte, his mother, and Harley just like family. Including Daphne.

After the twenty questions Mrs. Jackson asked Piper about Monte, she was convinced that he was not after Piper's money. Piper had told him and her family that a portion of her money was to be donated to the Cancer Institute that treated her. A small donation should be made to the hospital where she worked, and a trust fund set up for Harmony's first-born child, as she was to be the godmother if she could. But if not, it would be done posthumously.

Harley danced around the room, showing everyone what her next recital would be like.

"Hey Monte," Harmony said as she approached him. "Harley's adorable."

"Thank you." Monte replied.

"I'm in need of a flower girl for my wedding and I was wondering if you would mind letting Harley be my flower girl?"

"Yeah, sure thing. She would love it. Thank you for considering her."

"No, thank you for helping a sista out!"

"And thank you, again, Monte," Harmony said.

"For what?" he asked.

"For loving my sister," she said.

They hugged for a moment and separated when Piper arrived.

"Hey Harm. So, what do you think about Harley? Isn't she the cutest little thing?"

"Yeah, I was just thanking Monte for allowing her to be in our wedding. By the way, have you guys set a date?"

They looked at one another and Piper said, "Next weekend. Here at the house."

"Great. So, what's my role?" Harmony asked.

"It's only family and close friends, and we don't want it to be formal, so we won't have anyone standing with us. We only want to say our vows. Pastor Howard will be here to officiate, and then we will party the night away."

"I'm really happy for you, PJ," Harmony said. "I better go and find Jason and see what he's up to now." Harmony left.

"I have something for you, Piper," Monte said. He grabbed Piper's left hand and put her engagement ring on her ring finger. "I had to make it official," he said.

Piper smiled and kissed him on his lips. "That kiss was just as good as the first one," she said.

"I have a surprise for you. Once we get Dr. Cheung's approval for you to travel, we will take a small honeymoon."

"Wow, you are full of surprises tonight," Piper giggled.

When Harley finished her pre-recital for the Jackson family, her father invited her over. She had a question for Piper.

"Here is my final surprise for you this evening," Monte said.

He picked Harley up and turned her to face Piper. She asked, "Ms. Piper, when you and Daddy get married, can I call you Mommy?"

Piper's heart was full. She felt that if she died that moment, her life would have been complete. She held Harley's hand and kissed her on the cheek and said, "Yes, you can call me Mommy."

The night was full. Piper was ecstatic. She was as happy as she had ever been in life. For a minute, for just one little minute, she had forgotten that she had an incurable cancer and that she might not be with her family for long. She made a suggestion: "Let's celebrate life tonight. Let's party." And music began to play.

Mrs. Jackson and Daphne kept a watchful eye on Piper. They were sure she was overdoing it by dancing and singing. Brock Jr. caught them looking. "She's only having fun, Mom," he said.

"I know, but couldn't she be damaging herself? Making things worse?" Daphne said.

"What's life without living it?" Brock Jr. said. "Let her live and enjoy life while she still can."

Brock Jr. was right. No one knew how much time Piper had. Not the doctor, not Piper. No one. Piper saw them out the corner of her eye and couldn't believe the somber look on her mother's and Daphne's faces.

"Don't bring me down, please," she said to them. "Please be happy for me, because I am happy. Happier than I have ever been before in my life. So, stop looking that way. Come on, Mom, let's dance. Come on, Daphne."

The entire Jackson family was up dancing and celebrating that they were a family, a family with values. A family cut from the same cloth.

※

In the midst of the celebration, someone screamed from the center of the makeshift dance floor.

"My water broke!" Savannah shouted.

"Now?" Eric grabbed her by the arm and asked, "Is the baby coming? We need to go. You can't have the baby here. We have to go to the house and get the baby stuff, and then go to the hospital."

Savannah screamed again. "I don't think we have time for that! I can feel the baby's head between my legs. I need to lie down. I want to push it out!"

Piper instantly went into Nurse Mode: "Go get towels, blankets, and call 911. Hurry! Savannah have you been having contractions?"

"Yes, but they were so far apart, I didn't think I would be in labor until tomorrow." Savannah replied.

Mr. Jackson and Brock Jr. picked Savannah up and laid her on a lawn chair. Mr. Jackson asked that everyone go into the house, except for immediate family and Monte.

"Eric, go to the head and coach her like you did in class. We're going to deliver this baby," Piper said.

"Okay, baby, now push," Eric said, holding her hands.

Piper placed towels and blankets between her legs. She guided the baby's head as it left the mother's womb. As soon as the feet cleared, Piper grabbed the towel and covered the baby. But only after she took a peek at the baby's sex! "Congratulations, you two. You are the proud parents of Piper Jr."

No one had known the sex of the baby. They wanted it to be a surprise.

Monte was standing nearby and took Savannah's vitals as they heard the ambulance approaching.

Piper laid the baby across Savannah's chest. Savannah cried and said, "Thank you, Auntie PJ. You are the best aunt ever."

"I heard that!" Harmony yelled from the patio back door.

Savannah and Eric smiled and gazed at the miracle they had created.

That night made everyone realize how special their lives were, to be a part of this special family. They were grateful they had someone to share it with. They were happy for Piper. She was showing cancer a thing or two. She did not and would not let it stop her from living life to the fullest.

Brock Jr. made a decision that night, that he would spend more time with his wife, Ashlyn. He would no longer criticize her for not wanting to be eighteen again. They were older and not getting any younger. They had two children in college. They were proud parents.

Savannah and Eric were enjoying the birth of their baby girl and were ecstatic that Piper had been the one to deliver her.

But it would be the last night, at least for a while, that the Jackson family would be this happy. As the ambulance driver put Savannah on the gurney, and the paramedic got

Piper's information, Monte heard him ask Piper, "Ms., are you okay?"

Piper's mouth twisted upward. She began repeating herself, and then she went blank.

Chapter Thirty-Three

The stroke was on the right side of Piper's brain. It would be a few days before the doctors realized that the stroke was evolving.

Monte, and Mrs. and Mr. Jackson, all stayed with Piper for weeks, only leaving her side to change clothes, eat, and brush their teeth.

"Da," Piper said from her bed.

"Yes, baby? I'm here," Mr. Jackson said as he rushed to her bedside.

"I'm here, too," Mrs. Jackson said, following her husband.

Monte stood beside them.

"Goo, I'm not go yet," Piper managed to say.

"Don't talk. We're just happy you're doing better."

Weeks of therapy led to months of therapy, and finally, Piper regained her speech. Although still hospitalized, she was able to sit up in a wheelchair and talk.

During his lunch break, Monte attended her physical therapy sessions and convinced her that she would be all right.

"I will?" she asked.

"Of course. I'll be here to help you," he said. "The doctor said that if it hadn't been for the clot buster the ER doctor gave you, things would be much worse."

Piper gave Monte the thumbs up.

"Now, come on, let's do this."

Piper worked hard each and every day to regain her strength so that she could go home.

When he came the next day for physical therapy, he saw that Piper was dressed in a beautiful dress. Her sister Harmony was standing by her bedside with a white rose bouquet in her hand, Mr. Jackson standing on the other side. Brock Jr., Davon, and Daphne were also there with their spouses. Mrs. Jackson sat in the corner with Monte's mother and Harley.

"What's this?" he asked.

"We missed our wedding date, so let's do it now," Piper managed to say.

Monte was beyond surprised — he was thrilled. He walked toward the bed. Brock Jr. stopped him. "Wait," he said.

With Mr. Jackson and Davon helping her off the bed, Piper took five steps toward Monte by herself. Monte cried with joy.

They joined hands and the pastor performed the ceremony. Dr. Cheung and the nursing staff all witnessed the joyous occasion. When Pastor Howard pronounced them husband and wife, the room erupted in celebration.

Cake was served. When everyone was done eating, Mr. and Mrs. Jackson asked them to leave so that Piper could rest.

"Monte?" Piper said.

"Yes?" he answered.

"Will you stay with me until I fall asleep?" she said, exhausted.

He kissed her forehead and said goodnight.

Monte phoned his job, took the remainder of the day off, and spent it in the room with Piper, talking to her father. Mrs. Jackson took Monte's mother and Harley home.

"Monte, thank you for being a special person in my little girl's life. You are what she needs right now," Mr. Jackson said.

"I love her, Mr. Jackson," he said. "And thank you for trusting me with your daughter. She's a beautiful woman."

"Now that it's official, will you be taking her to your home, or will she be returning to ours?" Mr. Jackson asked.

"I'll let her decide," Monte responded.

Piper was released from the hospital a week later. She had made tremendous progress. She would resume her chemotherapy treatments soon. She was also given blood thinners to prevent clotting and another stroke. She had done everything the doctors had told her to do to recuperate one hundred percent. She was not one hundred percent, but she was much better.

Piper wanted to start living as husband and wife immediately upon her release. This was a new beginning, a new chapter in her life that she was surely looking forward to starting.

"May I carry you across the threshold, Mrs. DuVal?" Monte asked.

"I hope you don't break your back or pull a muscle," she said in return.

Careful with his words, Monte said, "I've been working out. I think I can manage."

He carried her into the house. A large banner that read "Welcome Home PJ" hung over the mantle. Mrs. Jackson was working with Mrs. DuVal in the master bedroom, preparing for Piper's arrival. Although she had recovered from the stroke, she needed to use a wheelchair, as well as oxygen at times.

Monte put Piper in the oversize leather recliner that was closest to the front door.

Mrs. DuVal had just finished cooking lunch and was setting the table. "Would you like to have lunch at the table or in the recliner?" she asked Piper.

"I'll eat at the table with everyone else," Piper said.

She placed her hands on the armrest and lifted herself from the chair. Mrs. Jackson was making her way to assist her. Monte gave her a quick nod no: Piper had to do it herself.

"That's right," Monte said. "Just as the therapist said, lift your body with the weight of your arms."

Mrs. Jackson didn't like it. Not at all. She was not used to being useless. She raised five children to become successful adults. She was there for them when they took ill. If they were hurt, she comforted them. Her daughter was recovering from a stroke — she had to help her. She rushed by Piper's side at the sight of a small wobble.

"I can do it, Mom. Please let me do it myself," Piper said.

"If you don't need me, then I'll just go home," Mrs. Jackson said.

Monte went to Mrs. Jackson and asked if they could speak privately. "Mrs. Jackson, with all due respect, Piper needs to do this herself. I know she wants you here for her, but she won't get any stronger unless she's able to do the physical work on her own. Your love for her is unmeasurable and she knows that. So please, stay and have lunch with us, as a family. Piper would really like that," Monte said.

Mrs. Jackson watched as her daughter struggled to walk to the chair at the massive dining table. Piper sat next to Harley. Harley reached over and grabbed Piper's hand and asked, "Can I call you Mommy now?"

Tears welled in Piper's eyes as she shook her head yes.

There was so much food that leftovers were guaranteed. Mrs. Jackson contributed to the lunch with her famous fried chicken and Mrs. DuVal did the rest.

Piper had a small portion — the same size as Harley. They held hands throughout lunch.

"Mommy?" Harley said shyly.

Feeling just a little awkward, Piper answered, "Yes?"

"Can I show you my room?" Harley asked.

"Sure, sweetie."

Monte gave Piper a questioning look. She shrugged.

"Harley, let's let Mommy ride in her chair to your room," Monte said.

Monte took the wheelchair to Piper. He led her to Harley's room.

"Aw, it's beautiful, Harley."

"This is where I keep my babies," Harley said, pointing to the baby dolls lined across her pillow.

"That's where I kept my babies, too, when I was a little girl," Piper said.

She was tired. Today had been physically and emotionally draining. "I need to lay down," she said to Monte.

"All right. How are you feeling?" he asked.

"Just a bit tired," she replied.

He escorted Piper to the master bedroom. He helped her with sitting on the bed. Even though they were married, Piper was a little shy about taking off her clothes while he was in the room. "Can you get my mother for me?" she asked Monte.

Mrs. Jackson rushed in the room.

"Mom, can you please help me get into my nightgown?" Piper asked.

"Sure, baby."

She helped her undress. She took out the new sleeping gown she had just bought for her as a wedding present.

"Do you need anything else, Piper?" Mrs. Jackson asked.

"No, Mom. I'm just a little tired. I'll see you tomorrow," she said.

"Get a good night's sleep," she replied.

Monte walked Mrs. Jackson to her car.

"I'll see you to tomorrow, Mrs. Jackson?" he asked.

"Yes. I'll stop by after you leave for work to help your mom with Piper," she said.

Monte felt his relationship with Mrs. Jackson would be more formal until she said "Call me Mom, Monte."

He smiled and gave Mrs. Jackson a hug.

Chapter Thirty-Four

After months of physical therapy and chemo treatments, Piper and Monte were given permission to take a honeymoon.

Piper was looking forward to the break in the chemotherapy treatments more than she was in having a honeymoon. The side effects hadn't been as bad as previous treatments, but they were still exhausting.

They decided to honeymoon not far from home and opted for Santa Barbara for a couple of weeks. The Cheshire Inn, Piper's favorite getaway spot.

They spent the week getting to know one another intimately. Piper's health was good. She hadn't needed to use the wheelchair or oxygen in a long while. She was getting along just fine.

The nights at the beach were the best part for her. The sun setting on the edge of the water, and Piper sitting in the sand between Monte's legs in a passionate embrace, were beyond happiness. She hadn't had this feeling in a long while.

Piper considered herself ninety-five percent back to normal. Her new treatments were working well, according to Dr. Cheung. She was ready to venture out and do more. She changed her eating habits and exercised daily. The tumors were shrinking, and her numbers were great.

Alone time with Monte was just what she needed. She needed to feel love. To be loved. To have someone hold her and be there for her. That's what Monte offered.

When they returned from the beach, they had dinner at the restaurant that sat right on the edge of the hotel. As they sat in the dim light in the back of the restaurant, Piper heard a familiar laugh coming from a nearby booth. A woman was cooing and a man was giggling.

Scott and Darla were having dinner. Piper decided to invite herself and Monte to speak to them. As they approached, Darla's eyes widened in surprise.

Scott stood and greeted them both. "What a surprise. Please, Piper, Monte, join us for dinner. I would really appreciate it if you would."

Monte turned to Piper to get her approval. She agreed.

Darla moved to the vacant seat next to Scott. Piper and Monte shared the bench directly across from them.

Darla reached across the table to grab Piper's hand and she accepted. Piper's smile was genuine. "So, what brings you guys to my favorite spot?" she asked.

Darla held out her left hand to show off the two-carat diamond wedding ring with a diamond studded wedding band to match. "We're on our honeymoon."

Piper and Monte laughed as if sharing an inside joke. Scott and Darla shared a puzzled look.

"We're on our honeymoon as well," Monte said.

And the table erupted in laughter.

They decided to celebrate together. Celebrate true love and the meaning of forgiveness.

Over the months of physical rehabilitation, Piper had rehabilitated her heart as well. She found time for forgiveness. To forgive Scott and to be satisfied with his decision. He wanted a family and now he had one. So did she.

They laughed over dinner and told stories.

"I'm a bit tired. I think Monte and I should call it a night," Piper said.

Darla stood, gave Piper a hug, and whispered, "You are a remarkable woman. Nothing but greatness will come to you. Thank you for being understanding."

Piper returned the hug and thanked her for the compliment.

She held Monte's hand during the short walk to the hotel room. "Piper, I love you and I am glad you're my wife." They hugged, shared a kiss, and entered the hotel.

As Piper began her nightly routine, she felt giddy. Monte was relaxing on the king size bed. The television was on a movie channel that Monte was only half focused on. He appeared to be in deep concentration.

Piper lay next to him. She kissed his cheeks, then his lips, then his neck.

Monte stopped her and said, "Come on, PJ. Let's not get something started that you can't finish."

Piper continued. She unbuttoned his shirt, still kissing his neck. "Who said anything about not finishing?" she said.

Monte relaxed and let his wife continue what she was doing.

Piper stretched her leg across his and sat up on him. "I think it's time we consummate this marriage!"

With nothing but joy on his face, Monte undressed his wife and made love to her for the very first time.

Monte was on top of the world the next day. They drove home, singing along with the oldies on the satellite radio.

"My dad called and wanted us to stop by for dinner tonight."

"Sure," Monte said, apparently distant.

"Is everything all right, Monte?" Piper asked.

"My world is perfect, now that you are in it," he said.

Piper smiled. "And what bought you to that conclusion?" she asked.

"PJ, you are an extraordinary woman. A woman of God. You are the virtuous woman God speaks about in the Bible. To overcome what Scott did to you, to forgive him and his current wife? You don't see stuff like that today. That just shows that what I thought about you was absolutely true. I am honored to be your husband." Monte raised her hand and kissed it gently as he drove home.

Piper sat back and let what he had said sink in. It was true. She had truly forgiven Scott and she believed she could now say what Monte wanted to hear. "I love you, Monte. I am so in love with you that if I died tomorrow, I would be completely satisfied with my life."

They held hands the remainder of the trip.

☙❧

Unpacking was a chore, and Piper hated it. She talked Harley into helping her. It gave her more time to spend with Harley.

"Mommy?"

Piper had to get used to being called that. "Yes, Harley?"

"I missed you and Daddy while you were on your honeymoon. Did you have fun? Did Daddy take you to see any animals like he does with me when we go on a trip?"

"No, we didn't see any animals. The next time we go, we'll take you with us!"

Happy, Harley ran out of the room, saying, "Nanny, Nanny, I'm going with Daddy and Mommy on their next honeymoon."

Piper laughed hysterically.

Mrs. DuVal entered the room and offered to assist Piper with the unpacking. "How are you feeling, darling?" she asked Piper.

"I'm feeling really good. Thanks for asking."

"We never really have had the chance to talk. Tell me a little bit about you."

"Well, this isn't my first marriage. I was married before and it just didn't work out."

"I don't mean that kind of stuff. Do you like to shop or cook? You know, girly stuff you like to do."

"Oh, shopping is my favorite pastime. And I'm okay with cooking. Prefer desserts, though. And I love shoes. I can buy shoes every day."

"Good. We'll plan a day and spend it shopping."

Piper hugged her mother-in-law. "Thank you."

"You are my only daughter. So, I'm glad we get to do some things together."

"Come on, guys, time to go to the in-laws," Monte said.

Dinner at the Jacksons' was in reality a surprise wedding reception for Piper and Monte. The Jackson family, as well as some of the DuVal family, would be in attendance.

Piper and Monte were beyond happy. The backyard was decorated in white and gold, with round tables with diamond and pearl centerpieces. *Exquisite* described the atmosphere.

Piper spent most of her time playing with baby Erica, Savannah and Eric's daughter. She shared a special connection to her. Delivering the baby had been the ultimate highlight of Piper's career.

The time came for speeches, and Mr. Jackson was the first to speak. "I would like everyone to help me welcome Monte to the Jackson family."

The backyard erupted in applause.

"I think it's time for the newlyweds to have their first dance," Mr. Jackson said.

They began a slow dance on the patio. Although they hadn't been together for years before marriage, the look in their eyes said love. Monte held his wife all so gentle in his arms, and Piper held the back of his head, as they shared a kiss.

Mr. Jackson grabbed his wife by the hand and escorted her to the patio to dance alongside their daughter. Brock and Ashlyn joined in as well. Before long, all the Jackson siblings were on the dance floor with their spouses.

It was a beautiful sight to behold. Piper felt as if she were in a fairytale. She couldn't believe that within a year, her life could go from sour to the sweetest life on Earth. She felt love from her family, she felt the love from Monte, and it was one that she would cherish forever.

ಬಿಎಸ್

During Piper's visit with Dr. Cheung, he gave her the best news she had had in a long time. "Ms. Piper, your numbers are great. You have made miraculous progress. Continue the medication that you were given."

Piper and Monte were thrilled to hear it. Just three months after her honeymoon, and she was feeling great.

Until one morning she felt nauseated. It wasn't the nausea she usually experienced after a chemo treatment. It was more like she'd eaten something that didn't agree with her.

She woke every morning for the next week, vomiting. Mrs. DuVal sat with her on the edge of the bed one morning after a bout. "Piper, how are you feeling?"

"I feel fine. I think it's the breakfast that I eat in the morning. It's not agreeing with my stomach. Or maybe it's the medication that I'm taking."

"Sweetie, I've seen this glow with my sisters and with Harley's mom. You're pregnant."

Chapter Thirty-Five

"WHAT?" Piper shouted. "You think I'm pregnant?"

"I know it. It's in your face. You're glowing," Mrs. DuVal said.

Piper jumped up and said, "Will you go with me to the clinic? I want them to test me. I don't want to take a home test the reading may not be correct. I want to be sure, to be positive, I have to find out. I have to find out today," Piper rambled.

"Sure. But don't you want to wait for your mom?"

"Yes, of course. She should be here shortly." Mrs. Jackson visited Piper twice a week for months, just to spend time with her daughter.

Once Mrs. Jackson arrived, they told her that they were going to the doctor so that Piper could have a test done.

"Has Piper been feeling ill lately?" Mrs. Jackson asked Mrs. DuVal while they waited.

"Just a little sickness, in the morning," Mrs. DuVal replied, hoping she would catch on, but she didn't.

Piper went into the back office and was handed a cup and asked to give a urine sample. The female doctor returned a while later to give Piper the news.

Piper went to the lobby, crying profusely. Mrs. Jackson ran to comfort her daughter. "Is everything all right Piper, what's wrong?" Mrs. Jackson asked.

Mrs. DuVal stood closely behind, smiling.

"Mom, I'm pregnant," she said through the tears.

Shock showed on Mrs. Jackson's face. "Pregnant? Oh, my Lord, Piper." Mrs. Jackson embraced her. Mrs. DuVal joined them.

Piper was radiant. She kept telling herself "I'm pregnant."

She had to think of a way to tell Monte. She wanted it to be clever. They decided to have a family dinner at the DuVals'. Piper would make her announcement then. She was on pins and needles the weeks leading up to the surprise.

The dinner was set for a Sunday, after church. The Jacksons and a few of Monte's family were all invited.

As dessert was being prepared, Mrs. DuVal asked Monte if he would take the pan out of the oven and bring it to the table.

He obliged. He returned with a tray of buns. The tray was not hot, and he was curious why a tray of buns was just sitting in a cold oven.

"Mom, are these done?" he asked.

Piper handed Monte a card and asked him to read it out loud. The card read: *We have a bun in the oven.*

"Bun in the oven," he read. "In the..." While everyone oohed and aahed, Monte was still trying to figure it out. He looked at Piper. She was making a circular motion on her stomach with her hand.

"You have a bun in your stomach?" he asked her, looking confused.

"Yes, we do," she said.

"You're pregnant?" he said.

Crying, she shook her head yes.

The family applauded.

Monte was in shock. He didn't know what to do. Finally, he grabbed his wife and kissed her passionately.

Once her grandmother explained to her that she was going to have a little sister or brother, Harley ran over to them.

Piper was content.

For the next few months, Monte treated Piper like an expensive china doll and Piper allowed it. Nothing mattered but the health and well-being of their baby. They made several doctor visits and medication adjustments.

During one visit, Harmony accompanied her. They hadn't spent very much time together, as Piper was enjoying her married life and Harmony was planning a wedding.

"How's the pregnancy going, Piper?" Harmony asked.

"It's going well. The doctor said my cancer is in a good place and the baby is doing well."

"I am so happy for you, PJ. You know there's only three months that separate you giving birth and my new wedding date."

"I'm aware of that. I have a plan. Mom got me a girdle to wear after the baby is born. I just don't like talking about it much."

"Why? You've beaten the odds. It's not every day that someone in your condition gets pregnant," Harmony said.

"I know. I just want a healthy baby. No complications."

"It will be the healthiest baby and look just like his Auntie Harm."

After the doctor's appointment, they had lunch and Piper made her way home. Monte was having the guest room cleared out and painted.

"What's going on in here?" Piper asked.

"The painters are painting the nursery," Monte said.

"Oh, that's a good idea. Having it done now gives it time to air out before the baby is born."

Piper went into the den to relax. She put her feet up and sat in the recliner. Harley came and joined her. "Mommy? Are you having a boy baby or a girl baby?" she asked.

"I don't know. We'll find out once the baby comes. Which one would you like?"

"I want a brother," Harley said.

"I will do my best to give you a brother," Piper said, smiling.

"How was your doctor's visit today?" Monte asked Piper.

"It went well. He changed my oral medication and I told him what we had decided to do about the chemotherapy."

He kneeled beside her and rubbed her pointy belly. "The baby's growing. This is nothing but one of God's miracles."

"Yes, it is. And I need you to promise me that, if it comes down to my life or the life of this baby, you choose this baby. My life span has been determined and I have since accepted my fate. You choose this child and love it, with every inch of you heart. Will you promise me that?" Piper asked.

He considered what Piper was saying. He could not fathom losing his wife, but he would honor her wish. "Yes, I promise. I pinky promise," Monte said. He kissed her on the forehead. "I'll leave you to rest now."

He retreated to the bedroom and prayed: *"God, I know thy will be done, but please spare my wife. She loves this child more than life itself. Allow her time with this child. In Jesus' name, I pray. Amen."*

He wept.

"Daddy, why are you crying?" Harley said. Monte hadn't noticed her come in.

"I'm just very happy that Mommy is having a baby."

"I'm happy, too, but I didn't cry. It makes me smile," Harley said.

"Come here, baby. I know you're not old enough to understand a lot about life, but sometimes things happen to people, and they have to go someplace else, and we won't understand why, but we learn to live with it."

"Like when my real mommy left me?" Harley said.

"Something like that. Just always remember that you are loved, and that no matter what happens, God has the final say."

"Yes, and we never argue with God's decision. Right, Daddy?"

"Yes, baby, that's right," Monte said. "Now go and check on grandma."

A thought crossed Monte's mind the instant Harley left the room. He had never considered having to tell his daughter that Piper died. How would he tell her? Where would the words come from when he didn't understand it himself?

Maybe Piper won't die. Maybe this baby is a sign that she's cured. Monte could only be hopeful as he thought about it.

Deep in thought, Monte hadn't noticed Piper standing over him. "Is anything wrong, Monte?"

"No, honey," Monte replied.

He grabbed her gently by the arm and rested his head softly on her stomach. "Be a boy, be a boy," Monte repeated.

Piper laughed. "If it is a boy, what will we name him?" Piper asked.

"He can be a junior," Monte said.

"What if it's a girl? Does she get to be a junior?" Piper asked.

"Sure. We'll name her PJ DuVal."

"I never thought about that. I like it," Piper said. She lifted his head and kissed him on the lips. "Your mom and I are going shopping. We should be back in time for a late dinner."

"You and my mom going shopping? I know I'm in trouble now. Don't let her teach you any bad habits," Monte said.

"We are only doing a little light shopping," Mrs. DuVal yelled through the door of Monte's bedroom.

൘൙

As they drove to the mall, Mrs. DuVal said, "Let's go to Abigail's Baby Store in Beverly Hills. They usually have a great selection of baby furniture."

"Sure," Piper said.

"As a wedding gift and baby shower gift, I want to buy all the baby furniture for the nursery," Mrs. DuVal said.

"Thank you. That's really sweet," Piper said. "But we've decided to wait until the baby is born to find out the gender."

"That's fine. Are you opposed to getting plain wood or white décor?" she asked.

"Not at all," Piper said.

As they shopped for décor, Piper couldn't help but notice the elegant taste Mrs. DuVal had.

"I really wanted a house full of babies when I got married. But it was not meant to be. That's why I invest so much into Harley. After my husband's death, I really just focused on raising Monte. I had help from my in-laws. They are very dear to me. If I go overboard just know I mean well."

"It's fine. You can do as much for us as you want,"

In the back corner they found a nursery with a zebra-like décor. It grabbed Piper's attention. The crib was white with a white dressing table. The dresser was a soft black. The stuffed animals were zebras and pandas. Black and white horses hung from the carousel over the crib. Stuffed black and white pillows lined the inside of the crib.

"What do you think about this one, Mrs. DuVal?" Piper asked.

"Yes, that's the one. It doesn't say boy or girl. It just says happy baby," Mrs. DuVal said.

They made the purchase and had a late dinner before returning home.

"Monte, we found the perfect nursery décor. Black and white animals," Piper told him.

"Wonderful. Did you and Mom have a nice time?"

"Yes. It was nice," Piper said. "It's really sweet of her to purchase the nursery."

"Yeah, it gives her pleasure to do it," Monte said.

"Now I need to see what I can let my parents do. My mom is so fussy when it comes to stuff like this."

"We'll figure it out," Monte said. "Oh, and by the way, Harmony phoned and asked if I would be in her wedding party. Someone had to back out. I told her sure."

"Yeah, she mentioned it this morning. I told her to ask you. Think I'm going to get to bed. I'm really tired."

"Good night, sweetheart."

Monte sat on the edge of his side of the bed and marveled at his wife. How beautiful she was there, carrying their child. He never thought this would be possible, but his dream had finally come true. He was married to the woman he thought was the most beautiful woman in the world, and now she was having his child. Life to him was at its best, and he could never be more grateful for what he had.

Chapter Thirty-Six

Now at eight months pregnant and in the best of health, Piper became more stressed about the health of her baby than ever. The doctor decided that she would have a Caesarean section.

During her final visit, she and Monte viewed the ultrasound and could not help but notice the gender of the baby and were happy. They would let everyone else be surprised. Everything was going as planned.

The morning of the big day, both families gathered for breakfast at Monte's home. They went in the family room after breakfast for pray. As they held hands, Mr. Jackson led them in prayer. He prayed for the health of his daughter and her newborn child. He prayed for the doctors' steady hands. He ended the prayer with everyone agreeing and saying Amen.

Mr. Jackson drove Piper and Monte to the hospital. Mrs. Jackson and Mrs. DuVal stayed behind to make sure the nursery was complete. After sanitizing the house from top to bottom, they left for the hospital as well.

In the waiting room, everyone was on pins and needles, awaiting the miracle baby's arrival.

Monte entered and made the announcement. "Welcome Monte DuVal Jr. Mother and baby are doing well. They are getting Piper ready for you guys to visit for a while."

"Monte Jr., huh?" Mr. Jackson asked.

"Yes, he looks very healthy and very handsome. They're going to run a lot of tests on him as well."

The nurse entered and told Monte that Piper was ready for visitors.

The family followed the nurse to Piper's room. Piper was sitting up, holding the baby. She was so mesmerized by the child that she didn't notice her family entering the room.

"Baby Monte? I would like to introduce you to your grandfather, Papa Jack, and grandmothers Nanny and Grandmother Jackson," Monte said.

"He's handsome," Mrs. DuVal said.

"Yes, he is," Mrs. Jackson said.

"He look just like his Papa Jack," Mr. Jackson said.

Monte sat on the edge of the bed admiring his wife and newborn son.

"Thank you," he said as he kissed Piper on her forehead.

"For what? A son?" she said, smiling.

"Yes, for our son. And for being my wife. You have made me the happiest and wealthiest man alive. Thank you. I love you with all my heart."

"Monte Jr., my angel," Piper said. "Want to hold him?" Piper asked Monte.

"Yes," he replied.

She placed him gently in Monte's arms as if he would break at the slightest touch.

Monte kissed his son and offered him to Mrs. DuVal. She held him for a moment and offered him to Mrs. Jackson.

Mrs. Jackson held him until she began to cry and handed him to Mr. Jackson.

"Come to Papa Jack," Mr. Jackson said. He rocked his grandson back and forth. He held the infant's tiny fingers. He kissed him and returned him to his mother.

"Come on, let's give Piper and the baby a break. We'll return tomorrow," Mrs. Jackson said. They all kissed Piper and Monte and said their goodbyes.

"You know, this baby here is a miracle?" Piper said.

"No. The miracle is you. You surpass all possibilities. This is the child God wanted you to have and now he's yours," Monte replied.

"Yes. I have a son. We have a son," Piper said tearfully.

"Honey, what's the matter?" Monte asked.

"I'm so happy right now. I always wanted a child, and now I have one. It doesn't matter what happens to me from this point on. I have a legacy and will live on in the lives of my children and grandchildren and great grandchildren," she said. "My life is now complete."

Monte kissed her on the forehead.

◆

When the Jacksons returned home, Mrs. Jackson could not control herself. She cried for hours. Mr. Jackson comforted her. "What's the matter, darling?" he asked.

"I'm happy for Piper. She has a child now. But I can't help but wonder at what cost? Is she going to be all right? Is her cancer worse because of this? I don't want to lose my child, Brock."

"Look, you know as well as I do the doctor said she was terminal. But she could live a viable life with lifestyle changes. It will be God's will, no matter what happens to her. Piper is a living miracle. Let's be happy for her."

"I want her to get better, Brock," she said, crying even harder now.

"Look at me, Madeline. I love you and we have to be strong for this family. Pull yourself together. We'll get through this."

She laid across his lap and cried.

The front door opened and Harmony walked in, yelling, "Anyone home? It's me. Harmony."

"Come on, Madeline, let's go downstairs. Wash your face. You don't want Harmony seeing you this way."

Mr. Jackson made his way downstairs and greeted his daughter. "So how much money do you need now?" he said jokingly.

"Aw, Daddy," she said as she hugged her father. "Mom and I are supposed to go shopping for her dress for my wedding."

"Good. She needs to get out the house and get her mind off things."

"Is she all right?" Harmony asked.

"Just a little emotional after seeing the baby."

"How's Piper and the baby doing?" she asked.

"Good. The doctor said that things are good with her and the baby. They should be home in a couple of days."

"Yeah, I spoke to her on the phone. She said give her some time before we come by and see the baby."

"Just picture me, two hundred and forty pounds lighter and with baby hair: That's Baby Monte," Mr. Jackson said.

Harmony laughed.

Mrs. Jackson made her way downstairs. "Are you ready, Harmony?"

"Feeling better, Madeline?" Mr. Jackson asked.

"Yes, Brock. I'm better. Let's go, Harmony."

"'Kay," Harmony said, noticing something obviously different about her mother.

Once in the car, Mrs. Jackson resumed crying.

"Mom, are you all right?"

"Yes, I'm sorry, Harmony. Just a little emotional about Piper."

"How was she doing when you saw her?"

"She's very happy and the baby is too cute. I'm just afraid it may have weakened her immune system."

"Mom, Piper has come to terms with whatever her fate maybe. She told me on the phone that she feels complete now, since the baby."

"I'm all right. Let's do some shopping. That should take my mind off things."

They went into Macy's and after hours of shopping, found the perfect dress for Harmony's wedding. Harmony dropped her mother off at home.

"Harmony, don't tell Piper how emotional I was. It will only upset her."

"I won't, Mom. I love you," Harmony said and pulled off.

Mrs. Jackson applied fresh makeup before entering the house.

She unlocked the door and heard smooth jazz playing in the family room. The smell of rosemary permeated the house. In the kitchen was a chef in his chef's attire, cooking.

"Hello?" Mrs. Jackson said with a little sarcasm.

"Hello, Mrs. Jackson. Please have a seat in the dining room. Mr. Jackson is waiting for you there."

East of the family room was the formal dining room. The large table that seated ten was now rearranged for dinner for two. There was a waiter dressed in white. He directed her to have a seat next to Mr. Jackson.

"Brock, what's all this?"

"Lately our life has been about our family. I've lost sight of my wife. Honey, I love you. For tonight, we are going back in time, before the children, to concentrate on us. If we're not strong in our love for one another, we will be no good to our family. I love you, Madeline, and I want us to renew our vows." Mr. Jackson stood, bent his right knee slightly, and presented his wife with a six-carat, princess-cut diamond solitaire ring. "Madeline, will you continue to be my wife, for as long as we shall live, through sickness and health, until death do us part?"

"Oh, Brock. I love you. Yes, I will continue to be your wife," she said.

Mrs. Jackson stood and hugged and kissed her husband. "My goodness, I have so much planning to do," she said.

"It's done. I've been busy all day. The ring was meant to be for your anniversary, but I thought you needed it now. I hired a planner and she's going to take care of everything. She sent the chef tonight. This was her suggestion. We are only inviting family and close friends. We have a suite for that evening at the Savoy Hotel and will spend the weekend there, then off to Hawaii for a week."

"Oh, Brock, this is wonderful. I'm so excited."

"Yeah, maybe we'll rekindle our romantic side," he said.

"Do you think it's a good idea to leave Piper?" Mrs. Jackson asked.

"I spoke to Monte and he knows. He said he would keep us posted on her and the baby."

"Great," she replied.

They began dinner with a salad, followed by the main course: rosemary and garlic roast beef with mashed potatoes and green beans. For dessert, crème brulée.

"I guess I need to go shopping. I'll make it a day with my girls. Thank you, honey, I really need this."

Mr. Jackson watched his wife get up from the table. *She just don't know how bad we both need this. This time, to get prepared for the worst*, he thought.

Chapter Thirty-Seven

The Jackson women gathered at their parents' home. Today was shopping day. A day to finalize the vow renewal and Harmony's wedding.

"Mom, I can't believe you let a wedding planner do the planning of your vow renewal," Daphne said.

"I don't mind. It gives me time to spend with the family. The older you get, the wiser you become. Besides, she has complete details as to how I want the day to go. She has the menu for the food, the flowers that I want, and the music. I'm still running things behind the scenes."

Her daughters all smiled.

"Piper, how's the baby? Getting big I bet," Daphne asked.

"He's wonderful."

"When will we get a chance to meet our new nephew?" Harmony asked.

"Soon," Piper replied.

Harmony looked at her sister. She was different. It wasn't that she was unhappy. She looked as if a part of her soul was missing.

As they sat in the back of the Jackson's Mercedes S550, Harmony slid her hand to Piper's and held it. She squeezed it tight, and a single tear spilled down Piper's face. And Harmony knew things were not the same.

They didn't speak, as they didn't want to say anything in front of their mother and Daphne. But Harmony knew.

Mrs. Jackson found the perfect dress in Sak's. Being an older woman, Mrs. Jackson had maintained her weight and was still shapely.

During dinner, they ate in silence — which was unusual while the four were together.

"Will you bring the baby to the party?" Mrs. Jackson said, breaking the silence.

"Yes, he'll be there. Mrs. DuVal will keep him with her so that we can all enjoy that day."

"PJ, do we have to wait to see him?" Daphne asked.

"Just until he has his first shots. You can stop by the house next week if you like," Piper answered.

Mrs. Jackson was quiet. She was listening to her daughters' conversation and realized it had been a long while since they had been together. Her day was complete. She was happy.

⋘⋙

Harmony couldn't contain herself. She had to know. She wanted to know what was going on with her sister.

After being dropped off at their parents' house, they went to the café around the corner.

"Is everything all right, PJ?" Harmony asked.

"No, Harmony. I want — No, I need you to be strong. I don't have much time left. The doctor said that it's getting close. I decided not to have chemo when I was pregnant with the baby."

"Why? Would it have harmed the baby?"

"It would be safe for the baby, if I had gotten in in my second or third trimester. I wanted a healthy baby. So much has happen in almost two years. I lost love, I found a new love, and I found an even greater love: being a mother. You can't ask for much more than that. And when I spoke to Monte about not taking the medication, he agreed with my decision. I told him that this baby's health was more important than mine. So, I opted not to do it."

"How much time do you have?" Harmony said through tears.

"A month or two, maybe less. We've known for a while now. Dad knows, which is why he's planning this celebration for Mom. Harmony, you have to promise that you won't say anything to anyone. We'll let everyone know sometime soon. Maybe when Mom and Dad return from Hawaii."

The sisters sat, held hands, and shed tears.

"I know I made the right decision, Harm. I just hope you and everyone else can be all right with that decision that I made."

"I'm not only losing my sister, I'm losing my best friend," Harmony said.

"Just pray for my soul. I would really love for you to do that. I'm fine with dying young. I've served my purpose and God has new plans for me now."

"Are you scared?" Harmony asked.

"Of course. I'm scared of the unknown. I have faith. I believe this is the plan God has for me."

"You are so strong, PJ. I love you."

"I love you, too. I don't think I'll be able to be in your wedding."

"If I know you, you'll be there in spirit. I'll be all right, PJ."

ଔଞ

No matter how tired she was nor how horrific the pain she suffered, Piper always had time for Monte Jr. and Harley.

She held her baby close to her body for as long as she could stand. Harley held the bottle as he ate, and Piper welcomed the help.

"How was your day today, hon?" Monte asked his wife. He kissed her forehead.

"Today was a good day, we had a great time with my mom. I told Harmony."

"How did she take the news?"

"She cried and then we talked about it. She's good now."

"Harley, go check on Grandma. I want to talk to Mommy."

Harley left the room, and Monte placed the baby in his crib. He sat next to his wife and began her nightly massage. He rubbed her neck, gently. Then her lower back.

Piper had been in excruciating pain since her sixth month of pregnancy. Her only goal had been to deliver a healthy baby — she didn't care at what cost. And that cost was her life.

Monte administered Piper's morphine after the massage.

"Do you have any regrets, Monte?" Piper asked.

"No, hon. I have you, and for any duration is a miracle to me." They cuddled on the daybed that rested across from Baby Monte's crib. "Do you have any regrets, PJ?" he asked.

"No, Monte. No regrets," Piper replied.

"What about your mom? You haven't told her yet."

"No. I can't," Piper said crying.

"Ah, baby," Monte said, holding her.

Piper cried a very long cry.

Chapter Thirty-Eight

The Savoy Grand Ballroom was decorated red and white. The theme: The Color of Love. Mr. Jackson was dressed in a white tuxedo. Brock Jr. and Devon in white suits. Mrs. Jackson wore a floor-length red velvet dress that clung to her waist. The Jackson women wore different shades of red.

Tables were adorned with red and white tablecloths. Red chair ties were draped over the white chair covers. Red rose petals and diamond-cut stones rested on diamond-shaped, mirrored centerpieces on each table. The festivities were in full swing. Everyone enjoying themselves. Mrs. DuVal left early with Baby Monte and Harley.

Piper took it easy that day. She didn't dance and didn't show too much emotion. She was in pain. Her body ached from head to toe, but the pain she had in her heart was unimaginable. She couldn't imagine not being here, in this moment, ever again. It was seeing her family celebrate love, the love her parents had for one another and the love they shared with their children and grandchildren, that got her through the evening.

The family photo of her and her siblings would be something great for them to remember her by. She stood next to Harmony. They secretly held hands. They shared that special bond, that special moment, for the final time.

After the family photo, Monte made their excuses and they headed home.

"Monte, I think the time is close. I feel so tired I only want to lay down and sleep. Please hurry. Get me home to see the baby and Harley.

Monte rushed through the traffic to get Piper home. "Do you want to go to the hospital?" he asked her.

"No, not yet. I want to say goodbye to my children."

He pulled into the circular driveway and parked in front of the door. Mrs. DuVal had just laid Harley down for the evening. Monte rushed through the door, carrying Piper, and startled his mother.

"Monte, what's wrong? Do you need me to call 911?"

"Yes, Mom. Please hurry."

Piper was near unconsciousness. He took her to the nursery and laid her on the daybed. He ran and woke Harley and sat her next to her.

Piper placed her arm around Harley's neck and said, "My sweet Harley, please always remember that I love you and that you were my very special daughter."

Rubbing the sleep from her eyes, Harley said, "Okay, Mommy, I love you, too."

Monte placed the baby in her arms. Piper cried. "I love you, my sweet baby boy. Know that I would do and make the same decisions for you again." She held him close to her heart.

Monte ran to the door when he heard the paramedics. Mrs. DuVal remained with Piper, holding her hand, saying a prayer for her.

Once in the ambulance, Mrs. DuVal called Mr. Jackson and gave him the news.

The hospital waiting room was filled with family in formal attire. Mr. and Mrs. Jackson were allowed to see Piper. They received the grim news that the time had come.

Piper was taken to a special room where family members were allowed to say their goodbyes. Daphne was beside herself. She could not understand how she could survive and Piper, being younger and more vibrant, couldn't. Her nieces and nephew all cried as they watched Piper struggle to breathe.

Davon and Brock Jr. held Piper's hand. Mrs. Jackson sat stoned-faced in the corner.

Harmony kissed her sister on the forehead and said, "Pinky promise kept."

Piper managed a brief smile and took her last breath.

The room erupted in tears. Mrs. Jackson sang the Lord's Prayer and the family joined her.

Monte was the last person to leave his wife. He had been strong for her for so long, he let out a loud cry. He rested his head on her chest and sobbed.

Brock Jr. walked over to him and picked him up from the bed. "It's going to be all right. We got you."

○§○

When Mr. and Mrs. Jackson returned from the hospital, Mrs. Jackson sat in the living room and stared at all of Piper's pictures.

"Come and sit down, Madeline," Mr. Jackson said.

"I'm fine, Brock. Really, I am. I knew the time was getting near. I looked at Piper when we went shopping and she was not herself. She looked lost. Her eyes were sunken in her head." She cried. "I knew. I knew my baby was leaving me, for good.

Mr. Jackson held his wife.

"Oh, Brock, it hurts so bad."

"I know it hurts. She's no longer suffering. Our child is at rest and she was ready," Mr. Jackson said, crying.

"I can do this," Mrs. Jackson said. "I can. She would not want me to cry like this." She dried her tears. She kissed her husband and went upstairs.

Mr. Jackson took her place. He stood and looked at Piper's pictures. He decided that he would shed his last tear, right here and right now. With every tear that fell, his crying increased. Louder. Harder. He felt he needed to hit something, someone. It became unbearable.

Mrs. Jackson returned with a handkerchief. She held her husband and said, "We will get through this. God help us!" she yelled.

ॐ

Piper died on a Saturday. Her funeral was set for the following Saturday. She had arranged everything: the church, the Gospel singing group that sang on Sundays at the church. She wanted Brock Jr., Davon, Sherman, Jason, William her nephew and Eric, her nephew-in-law to be her pallbearers. She had written everything down and made the necessary contacts.

She had written her own obituary: *Piper Destiny Jackson was one of Brock and Madeline Jackson's beautiful daughters. She accepted Christ at the age of sixteen and was baptized. She made a habit of reading scripture every evening to make sure she made her connection with God daily.*

She had a passion for helping people and became a nurse.

Her childhood sweetheart, Scott Evans, was her first husband. They were married for five years and decided it was best to part ways.

Monte DuVal fell in love with Piper before she knew he existed. She felt a connection to him when they finally met, and they married shortly thereafter.

Piper lived life vivacious life. She gave her life for her child.

She leaves to cherish her memory: Husband Monte; children Harley and Monte Jr.; parents Brock and Madeline Jackson. Mother-in-Law Claire DuVal; Her sisters Daphne and Harmony. Her brothers Brock Jr. and Davon. Many nieces and nephews, aunts, uncles, and cousins.

She asked that everyone remember her spirit and not spend their days mourning her. She wants you to promise. (Pinky Promise!)

Her celebration of life was beautiful. The repast was held at Daphne's home. They shared so many pleasant stories of Piper's courageous feats.

In lieu of flowers, the family honored Piper's wish and asked that donations be made to The Cheryl Lincoln Research and Oncology Center.

During the repast, Scott and Darla made their way to pay their respects to the family. "The service was beautiful, Mr. Jackson," Scott said, shaking his hand.

"Piper was a very special person, very courageous. I really admired her," Darla said.

The Jacksons thanked them for coming and retreated to the house where the immediate family were waiting in the living room. "We're going home. I'm exhausted," Mrs. Jackson said.

"Yes. We'll see you guys Sunday, for dinner," Mr. Jackson said.

They were silent during the ride home. The house was still. An unnerving feeling fell over Mrs. Jackson when she opened the door. She called a cleaning service to schedule a deep cleaning.

"Madeline?" Mr. Jackson yelled.

"Yes, Brock?" she replied.

"I want to give our Hawaii trip to Harmony and Jason as a wedding gift. Are you all right with that?"

"Yes, Brock. I know they would really like to have a honeymoon. We've been so busy, I forgot the wedding is in a couple of weeks. I'm looking forward to the wedding."

"Yes. It would be nice to be surrounded by our family."

Chapter Thirty-Nine

The off-white dress Harmony wore fit perfectly. Mr. Jackson whispered in her ear, "Are you ready for this day?"

"Yes, Daddy. I'm ready. PJ is here with me in spirit. I feel her."

The groom and best man entered the church. The music began and the wedding party made their entrance. Harmony's niece Sabrina and Jason's brother Roderick entered the sanctuary. Next was Monte, walking alone. He made his way to the altar, placed a bouquet of roses where Piper would have stood.

Harley and Jason's cousin, the ring bearer made their entrance next.

The wedding guests stood as Harmony made her way into the church.

Jason smiled as his new bride walked the length of the church. Mr. Jackson gave him her hand. They stood in front of the priest and said their vows.

During the wedding reception, Mr. Jackson gave Harmony and Jason their gift: an all-expense paid trip to Maui, Hawaii, along with a $2,000 gift from Piper.

They were shocked and beyond thrilled. Piper had never said she was leaving them a gift.

The honeymoon was the following Saturday. The flight was peaceful. Jason was a sweetheart. He pampered Harmony from the time she said "I do."

In the hotel, Harmony showered and then waited for Jason to shower so that they could begin touring the island.

Before she got dressed, an overwhelming feeling came over her. It was like a rush of air with a turbulent undertow.

She decided to do it. She laid her head on the pillow and with her breast exposed, she took her right hand, placed it under her head, and massaged her left breast. Satisfied that she felt nothing, she did the same with her right breast. The right breast did not feel like the left, and she became nervous. Not knowing exactly what to look for, she ran her right hand over her left breast again to memorize the feeling. The right breast was different. She stood up in shock.

Jason exited the bathroom and noticed that Harmony was standing in the middle of the floor, nude.

"Couldn't wait?" he asked her.

"No, Jason. I felt a lump in my right breast."

The End

Made in the USA
Columbia, SC
07 February 2023